OTHER YEARLING BOOKS YOU WILL ENJOY:

SUGAR BLUE, *Vera Cleaver*
THIMBLE SUMMER, *Elizabeth Enright*
THE SATURDAYS, *Elizabeth Enright*
THE FOUR-STORY MISTAKE, *Elizabeth Enright*
THEN THERE WERE FIVE, *Elizabeth Enright*
SPIDERWEB FOR TWO, *Elizabeth Enright*
PHILIP HALL LIKES ME. I RECKON MAYBE., *Bette Greene*
GET ON OUT OF HERE, PHILIP HALL, *Bette Greene*
AUTUMN STREET, *Lois Lowry*
THE HOUSE WITHOUT A CHRISTMAS TREE, *Gail Rock*

YEARLING BOOKS/YOUNG YEARLINGS/YEARLING CLASSICS are de-
signed especially to entertain and enlighten young people. Patricia
Reilly Giff, consultant to this series, received the bachelor's degree
from Marymount College. She holds the master's degree in history
from St. John's University, and a Professional Diploma in Reading
from Hofstra University. She was a teacher and reading consultant
for many years, and is the author of numerous books for young
readers.

For a complete listing of all Yearling titles, write to
Dell Readers Service, P.O. Box 1045,
South Holland, IL 60473.

Night Cry

by
Phyllis
Reynolds
Naylor

A YEARLING BOOK

Published by
Dell Publishing
a division of
Bantam Doubleday Dell Publishing Group,
666 Fifth Avenue
New York, New York 10103

With special thanks
to Sharon Bernstein,
Atticus
and Bulldozer

The trademark Yearling® is registered in the U.S. Patent
and Trademark Office.

ISBN: 0-440-40017-1

Reprinted by arrangement with Atheneum Publishers,
a division of Macmillan Publishing Company

Printed in the United States of America

January 1988

10 9 8 7 6 5 4 3

CW

To my editor,
JEAN KARL,
in appreciation

Night Cry

One

FEAR, like icy pellets, rained down on her as Ellen entered the barn. In the sudden darkness she could not see him, but she knew that Sleet was there.

She waited until her eyes had adjusted, then slowly made her way across the bare earth floor, scanning the tools, the feed sacks, the corners. A noise—a shifting, a hoof sound—turned the skin on her arms to gooseflesh.

The dark horse stood in shadow, watching her come. He sidled about, wheezing, nostrils flared. Just as Ellen reached the stall, he lifted his head high above her, and the brown pupil rolled in the white of his enormous eye. Ellen felt caught in its sweep.

Turning, she fled back through the barn and plunged into the brightness of the late July sun.

I won't go there again, she told herself. *That's the last of it.*

"Ellie?" Her father stood on the porch steps. "You fixing to make breakfast?"

Ellen crossed the clearing, which lay near the top

of the ridge. It was in this rugged corner of Mississippi that the hill country began, where narrow twisting roads led to cabins above or below.

"The red hen's been in the barn again, and I can't find her egg," Ellen said.

Joe Stump followed his daughter inside. "We'll make do," he told her, and poured the coffee.

"Dad, this is crazy, taking turns each morning, who gets an egg. I'm going to start ordering some from Gacy's."

Ellen's father smiled as he settled himself in his chair. "Probably a couple eggs out there if you look in the right place. Red hen's taken a fancy to Sleet. They're in his stall, I'll bet."

"I'm not going in there again," said Ellen. She took the cornbread from the old wood stove and carried it to the table, avoiding her father's eyes.

The kitchen was quiet except for the sound of Joe's spoon, gently stirring in his cup.

"It's been over a year now, Ellen April," he said finally, "and it weren't the horse's fault."

"I won't go near him," Ellen repeated, and pulled her chair up to the table.

They sat across from each other, and Ellen was conscious of how much she resembled her father in her old shirt and jeans. They had the same long, lean, elastic look; the same oversized hands and feet; same hair, the color of mahogany. But Joe's face was as weathered as a barn door while Ellen's was smooth.

It wasn't eggs they were arguing about. While it was wasteful not to collect the ones in the barn, they could afford to order some now and then. The horse was the problem. It was Sleet.

Ellen watched as her father reached into the pan and scooped up a square of cornbread. When he tried to butter it, it crumbled in his hand.

"No egg in that either," Ellen said wryly.

Joe stuffed it in his mouth anyway and winked at her. "Well, what'll we do, Ellie? Give up the farming life? Get us one of those condominium things like they got in Oxford?"

Ellen rested her head on her hand and made a teasing face. "With a swimming pool, I suppose?"

"Sure. Tennis court, too."

"Don't have any bathing suit."

"We'll get you one."

"Never held a tennis racket in my life."

"Time you learned."

"Huh. We go getting all fancy like that, Dad, and I got to have me a coming-out party like the girls in Jackson do."

"What kind of party is that?"

"You know—where they all wear long dresses and their fathers walk them around a ballroom and introduce them to everybody."

"*Introduce* 'em?" Joe said. "Where they been all this time, those girls? Locked in the basement?"

They laughed together.

"I don't want any condominium," Ellen said. "Wouldn't even know how to act." She reached over and began stacking the dishes, then rose and took them to the sink. "Just don't ask me to go near Sleet, that's all."

Her father went across the hall to change, and Ellen stood at the kitchen window, arms folded loosely over her chest. There were no houses as far as she could see—just trees tangled with muscadine vine and kudzu. Kudzu grew so fast in Mississippi, it was said, that if a man parked his car at a railway station Friday evening and didn't get back till Monday, he might not find it at all.

It was the way Ellen felt sometimes herself: as though kudzu had crept up here to this backwoods place, along the fences and telephone wires, and had covered her completely. Who even knew she was here, except for a handful of friends from her eighth-grade class, a teacher or two, and the folks that lived at the junction?

To the right of the clearing, beyond the camellia bush, was the path that led to the bluff. Up there, beneath a chinaberry tree, was her mother's grave, marked by a quartz stone she used to keep on the window ledge to see the sun shine through. For five years Ellen, her father, and Billy had gone up the hill every Sunday and pulled at the weeds, polished the stone, and watered the roses that Ellen had planted. And then, on a day dark with thunder, Billy had been buried there beside his mother.

Ellen was conscious of her father in the kitchen again, wearing his green suit and the brown tie that had shrunk in the wash. He stopped at the sink and ran the scrub brush over his knuckles, then picked up his sample case near the door.

"Tell Jimmy-Clyde I'll pay him three dollars a week to tend the horse," he said. "You tell him that when he brings the groceries next time, hear?"

"Be cheaper to sell the horse," Ellen answered.

"You tell Jimmy-Clyde what I said," her father repeated, and went on out to the car.

Jimmy-Clyde was fourteen, a year older than Ellen, but his mind seemed to have stopped growing at about the age of eight. He was delivery boy for Mrs. Gacy's small grocery, and twice a week rode his bicycle up the long dirt road to Joe Stump's mailbox and then a quarter-mile in on the deeply rutted lane to the house. Only Jimmy-Clyde would have done so without complaint.

"*Re*-tard! *Re*-tard!" Children had taunted him once down in Millville as Ellen watched horrified from the steps of the post office.

And Jimmy-Clyde, plodding along, arms dangling, had turned and faced his accusers.

"I know enough to keep my mouth shut," he retorted, repeating what his father had taught him to say. And Ellen clapped, much to Jimmy-Clyde's delight.

Ellen was sitting on the front porch when he rode up around eleven with the order she had phoned in. She sat in the very center so as to catch the breeze channeled along the open hallway leading from front to back—a "dog-trot cabin," some called it, because a dog could trot right through. The two bedrooms were on one side of the hallway, kitchen and parlor on the other.

Turbo, the yellow dog, rose up when he heard the bicycle and moved to the edge of the porch.

"Hi!"

Jimmy-Clyde always called out before he came into view. Still hidden by lilac and the leathery magnolia leaves, he announced his arrival in a high-pitched voice.

"Hello, Jimmy-Clyde," Ellen called back, and finally there he was, riding across the grass, panting, the deep basket in front holding the groceries.

His face was as flat as a dinner plate, his upper eyelids folded. He had a small round head and short arms, and when Ellen had first seen him several years back, she had thought he was from a different country altogether. Later, when she got to know him, she decided that for Jimmy-Clyde, it *must* be like living among strangers in a foreign land.

"No bread today!" he said, getting off the bicycle and carefully lowering the kickstand. "No bread today because you know why? Because the truck didn't come. Mrs. Gacy says you'll get it Thursday."

"We can manage," Ellen said, holding the parlor screen open for him.

"You'll get it Thursday," Jimmy-Clyde repeated. He hurried toward the house, his thick hands with the short fingers curled tightly around the bottom of the sack. Every so often his tongue darted out between his lips. He kept smiling at Ellen.

When the sack was on the table, Jimmy-Clyde went through his usual ritual of taking every item out, one at a time, and calling it by name. He had obviously memorized every product in Gacy's store and was enormously proud of his accomplishment. Ellen waited.

"Nabisco shredded wheat," Jimmy-Clyde chanted, placing the box on the table upside down, then noticing and putting it right side up. "French's mustard . . . hamburger . . . Pillsbury flour. . . ."

"You did fine," Ellen told him when he was through. "You got everything."

"All but the bread," said Jimmy-Clyde. "You'll get that Thursday."

"You want some Kool-Aid?" she asked.

Jimmy-Clyde beamed in reply.

Ellen poured a glass for him from the refrigerator, and they moved on out to the porch. The boy drank it thirstily, then flicked at the droplets around the rim with his tongue. A bee moved in and out of the wisteria growing on the trellis.

"Can I see the horse now?" Jimmy-Clyde asked finally, as Ellen knew he would.

"Yes," she told him. "Listen, Jimmy-Clyde. My dad said to tell you: if you'll tend the horse when you're here each time, he'll pay you three dollars a week. I don't think Mrs. Gacy would mind if you stayed a little while."

Jimmy-Clyde stared at her, and a slow smile spread across his face, making a second chin.

"A job?" he said.

"That's right. Shovel out the stall and put down fresh straw. You've done it before, but now you'll get paid for it. Dad quit work at the gas station last week and got himself a traveling job. Won't have as much time to take care of things as he used to."

"Wow," said Jimmy-Clyde, still beaming. He continued to sit there and smile at her.

"You can begin now if you want," Ellen suggested.

"Okay!" Jimmy-Clyde lurched forward eagerly and started toward the barn.

～～～

The Stumps's cabin faced the clearing and the barn and pasture beyond. There was a sassafras tree growing near the front steps, a huge beech in the yard. Sycamores stood ghost-white on the right side of the house, blocking the view of the bluff, and on the left, pecan trees rained down yellow pollen in spring from tassel-like blossoms, covering porch and steps. Beyond the pecans was the vegetable garden running the length of the lane. There was nothing behind the cabin but a forest of cucumber trees, so tangled and thick that the back stoop was always in shadow. Ellen preferred the front.

She sat now, however, with her hands thrust up the sleeves of her checked shirt as though she were cold, uncomfortable with herself. Turbo had followed Jimmy-Clyde out to the barn and stood wagging his tail in the doorway. Ellen watched.

It wasn't as though they really needed Jimmy-Clyde. Sleet was a pasture horse and used to grazing in the field. Between the creek and the meadow, he could get along all right until Joe could get around to shoveling out his stall or giving him a special treat of oats. That wasn't what Ellen's father had in mind, however. Jimmy-Clyde was someone who would talk to Sleet, stroke him, rub him down—all the things Ellen would not—could not—bring herself to do.

She had no fear for Jimmy-Clyde in the barn. Evil bounced off the boy like a drop of water on a hot griddle. Even Sleet couldn't penetrate the innocence. He always stood still when Jimmy-Clyde was about— never neighed, never kicked. The searchlight eye remained quiet.

Ellen sucked in her breath. She could remember when the horse had first arrived at their house. Her father bought him for thirty dollars from a man down at the junction. The horse was to be a Christmas present for Billy who was ten at the time—the only thing he wanted—had ever wanted.

Ellen and Billy had watched from the window as their father walked the horse up the lane in a cold, icy drizzle. The animal clopped along behind him, head to one side, tossing his mane every so often and snorting with displeasure, his coat covered with a shiny glaze.

"It's sleet!" Billy had said when he saw it, and somehow the name stuck.

"He's storm-shy," Joe had told them in the barn as they dried the horse off. "Don't mind rain much, but he's spooked by thunder. Good horse, the man said, if you go out with him on a clear day. Best I could do for thirty dollars, Billy."

Billy hadn't cared. Sleet was the first thing on his mind when he got up in the mornings, the last thing he tended to before he went to bed. If the horse was sick, Billy slept out in the stall all night to be near him.

And then, a year ago, on the back trail up from Granny Bo's, Sleet had bolted there in the woods and thrown Billy headlong into a gully.

Ellen still remembered the way the big animal had come pacing into the clearing, its eyes wild, body taut, and the saddle empty. She had rushed up the path to the bluff, then down the trail on the other side as thunder cracked overhead. When the storm hit and rain washed down the dirt hillside, she went on, slipping and sliding toward the big rock in the gully. And it was there she found her brother just above the place where the ginseng grew, his neck broken. Dr. George said he was dead before he ever reached the hospital.

"It's the devil," Granny Bo told Ellen when she

heard about it. "The devil come out of old man Keat when he died and went in that horse. They don't die off, them spirits, they finds them somethin' else."

It was never the same again with Sleet—not for Ellen. The horse had run wild in the pasture that day until Joe Stump came home, and it took three neighbors to corner the animal and bring him in.

Long into the night, Ellen and her father had sat together, mourning Billy.

"Let's have Sleet put away." Ellen had wept.

"Weren't the horse's fault, Ellen April," Joe said, wiping his eyes. "Billy knew he shouldn't take him out with a storm comin'. He knew that, and he oughtn't to have gone."

"How can you talk like that?" Ellen cried out. "Billy's dead! I'll tell you what *we* ought to do—ought to have the horse shot."

"You think that would make things right, us puttin' a bullet to Sleet?" her father asked, grieving. "Only way I can hang onto my boy at all, Ellen, is to hang onto that horse—the way Billy would have wanted."

And so the demon horse stayed, but evil seemed to reach out for Ellen whenever she came near him— clutched at her with scratchy fingers and clawed at the skin on her arms. It was as though Ellen could hear the rasp of the devil's breath in the horse's whinny, smell the stink of devil's dung in the warm manure. Whenever she approached the stall, her fear went before her and riled the horse, so that when they confronted each other, eye to eye, he wasn't a horse at all.

Two

THE HAMBURGER was wrapped in butcher paper and then again in the society section of yesterday's *Evening Times*. It was Jimmy-Clyde's job to wrap all the meats well before he delivered them and, at Ellen's request, he always wrapped her order in the news or society pages.

She spread them out on the table as she made her lunch. In the lower right-hand corner there was a picture of a bride in a big white hat, and Ellen scanned the write-up while she ate a cheese sandwich:

> . . . The bride is an 11th generation descendant of William Tyler of Norfolk, Virginia, who was born in York, England, and emigrated to America in 1675. She is also a direct descendant of James Fairfield, who was active in the patriot cause in Virginia before the American Revolution. . . .

"My, my!" Ellen said dryly.

She tried to imagine her own picture in the *Evening Times,* assuming she were to be married tomorrow, which she wasn't. The most interesting thing she could think of to say about her ancestors was that her great

Uncle Virgil had owned a chicken farm near Yazoo City.

Ellen April Stump, grandniece of chicken farmer, marries local boy. . . .

She laughed out loud and read the rest of the paper. The big news was that the famous film producer, Robert L. Cory, who had been born in Millville, was coming back to dedicate a new auditorium. There was a picture of him, his young wife, and their four-year-old son. "Millville to Welcome Its Own," the headline read.

What was it like to go away and then come home, all different? Ellen wondered. Or to have a father so famous that everybody knew his name? "The Cory Auditorium," engraved letters over the door would read, and forever after folks would know that Cory was somebody special.

She glanced at the clock as she heard Jimmy-Clyde's footsteps in the open hallway. Four minutes till noon.

"All done," he called.

"Good," Ellen said.

"I gave him water," said Jimmy-Clyde. "I gave him water in a bucket. So he doesn't have to go all the way down to the creek."

"That's fine," said Ellen. "Thanks a lot, Jimmy-Clyde." He beamed.

As the rattle of his bicycle sounded on the lane again, Ellen went into the parlor and turned on the TV. This was the time of day in all the long, humid months of summer that she liked best. She didn't want to be a bride in a picture hat in the *Evening Times* or a film producer from Los Angeles. If Ellen had an idol at all, it was Maureen Sinclair, on *News at Noon,* for channel WMER out of Merwyn City.

For a while there wasn't any picture at all. Ellen shook the set back and forth a few times, then jiggled the antenna. A faded image in black and white flickered across the screen with the familiar beep that signaled the news.

"*News at Noon,*" the announcer said, "with Maureen Sinclair."

And there she was, a poised young woman with thick black hair and beautifully tapered eyebrows. Whenever something happened, anywhere at all in the world, Ellen was thinking, Maureen Sinclair knew about it. Name an important person, and Maureen Sinclair knew who that person was. Ask her about an earthquake in Turkey, and she could tell you in a moment. To be so in touch with other places, that was what Ellen envied. She wanted to get outside her own skin, to be a part of something larger than herself. And yet . . .

The sound went off. There was Maureen Sinclair, her mouth silently opening and closing, and then there were pictures of fighting somewhere, possibly the Mideast. Maureen Sinclair again, and then pictures of a helicopter landing in a desert, followed by a protest march of strikers in Michigan. Ellen got up and banged the set.

The sound came on as a man in a white suit gave the stock market report, and then it was Maureen Sinclair once more.

"Locally," she said, "work was completed yesterday on the new auditorium in Millville, a gift of film producer Robert L. Cory. The auditorium will be formally presented to the town next month by Mr. Cory himself, and gala festivities are planned. 'I have been looking forward to this for a long time,' Mr. Cory said, upon being told that the auditorium was finished. 'I want Millville to see some of the same productions that folks in New York and Chicago get to see.'" Maureen Sinclair smiled into the camera and folded one hand over the other. "Well, it may not turn Millville into Broadway, but one thing is certain: there are going to be some exciting times coming up in the months ahead. This is Maureen Sinclair, saying good afternoon from WMER."

The television set, which was older than Ellen herself, buzzed ominously, and she got up and turned it off.

"This is Ellen Stump, saying good afternoon from WMER," she practiced. Then, "This is Ellen April Stump. . . ."

The "April" didn't help.

She went outside and fed the crust of her sandwich to Turbo, then crossed the clearing and headed up the path toward the bluff. She wouldn't mind a little Broadway in her life, she was thinking. Once, when Mother was still alive, the whole family had gone to Merwyn City to see *The Music Man* put on by the local high school. Ellen had thought about it for weeks afterwards. She couldn't even imagine herself getting up in front of a bunch of people and opening her mouth, but she sure didn't mind being in the audience now and then. She didn't mind that at all.

Of the five acres owned by her father, only the pasture was fenced in. Yet there were just four ways that a person might leave or enter the Stump property: the rutted lane leading to the road; the path up the bluff and down the other side to Granny Bo's; a left turn at the top of the bluff to the old Brody place, now deserted; and a gate at the end of the pasture, a shortcut to the Brodys'.

Everywhere else, the land was enclosed by a wall of vine, so dense and dark that trees leaned with its weight. It matted the underbrush, making an impenetrable net of leaves and branches. For as long as Ellen could remember, the closed-in feeling had given her a kind of security, defining her boundaries, setting a limit on where she need go. But there were other times, especially in the last year or two, when she had felt uncomfortably trapped, as though the familiar things that had brought such comfort before had turned on her sharply and become the wardens of her own prison.

The path grew more steep and rocky once she had passed the fork leading to the chinaberry tree, but Ellen climbed on until she reached the top. There, a huge box elder—struck three times by lightning—spread out in all directions. The yellow dog, tagging along beside her, went dashing off through the plum bushes and silver grass in search of a scent.

A long rope, knotted in places, dangled limply from a lower branch of the box elder, and Ellen deftly hoisted herself up, hand over hand, until she reached the lookout she and Billy had made. Two rusty dinette chairs, one with a leg missing, had been wedged securely between the branches. Ellen climbed onto one and propped up her feet.

Here, they used to pretend—she and Billy—that they could see their whole "kingdom" and would take turns parceling out the land; if Billy chose the river, Ellen got the creek; if Ellen got the valley, Billy got the ridge; if Billy got the hickory grove, Ellen would choose the woods beyond. . . . Last to be chosen always was the old Brody place, down in the ravine. The porch roof had caved in on one side. Now and then squatters would take it over for a week or a month, but they'd soon move on, leaving it to the field mice once again. Mostly it was kudzu as far as the eye could see.

"I'm never going to leave here," Billy would say, his round face serious. They would be chewing on pepper grass, biting the seed. "Even if I get married, I'm going to keep on living here."

Ellen would drape her legs over the branches of the box elder and say, teasing, "I'm going to marry first."

"Then I'll build a house right beside yours, and we can share," Billy would answer.

"I get the stove," Ellen would say as they began dividing the contents of the house. She always chose the stove. She could remember once when her father brought home a big flat box of baby chicks, shoving it beneath the stove, between its stubby iron legs, to keep them warm until morning. Mittens were hung to dry over the hot surface, and toast grilled on the taps above the fire box. The oven itself, large as a cave, could hold two turkeys baking at the same time.

"Will *you* ever leave here?" Billy would ask finally, the question always at the back of his mind. It was something he asked more frequently after their mother died.

"What's there to leave for?" Ellen would say by way of answer. "Everything I want is right here."

And for the most part, Ellen had meant it. It was a sticking-together kind of feeling back then. There was something comforting about living in the same house her father had been born in, with the memory of her grandparents, now dead, and the nicks and scratches of several generations of Stumps before her.

But after Billy died, the vine-heavy trees took on a sinister look; the rooms of the small house seemed more narrow, the walls moving in. The horse that she and Billy used to ride with such pleasure seemed a messenger from some silent evil master. It was as though fate had pointed one long gray finger at this small place up on Crow's Point. The breeze in the magnolia trees and the rustlings in the pomegranate bushes became the whisperings, instead, of Granny Bo.

On Wednesday, Ellen went to see the old woman. Her real name was Alma Goff, and how she got to be called Bo, she didn't even remember herself. She lived "two miles back of the backwoods," as folks at the junction put it. The cabin had been built by her first husband and lived in by husbands two and three. Now there was only Granny Bo left, and she was in her eighties.

It was almost a forty-minute journey to her cabin, and the Stumps were the closest neighbors she had. Granny Bo had no phone—no electricity at all.

"If she fell," Ellen's mother used to say, "she could lie there a week before anyone found her. It's up to us to look in."

That had been one more reason for buying Sleet. Sure-footed, the horse had clambered up the rocky path to the bluff, down the other side, and then galloped over the gentler hills below, making the journey in fifteen minutes. Ellen had learned to ride well. She had taught herself to hug the horse with her knees and keep her balance, letting the reins hang loose on a downward slope, trusting the horse's judgment to take the right step. But she would not ride him now, the horse with the wild eye and demon whinny.

Thistles scratched against the legs of her jeans as Ellen edged down the path, her feet pushing hard against the toes of her sneakers. Turbo would go a few feet and look back to make sure she was coming, then sniff out another length of trail. Ellen carried a loaf of blueberry bread and some sassafras bark so that they could make tea when she got there. Oak trees, heavy with vine, made the ground dank beneath them, and ferns thrived in the moistness.

Despite the long trek, there was something about Granny Bo that drew Ellen to her—something in the woman's proud independence that matched her own. The things Alma said, however, were a different matter. Ellen tried to laugh them off, but never quite succeeded.

Granny Bo was watching for her when Ellen reached the cabin. Ellen never managed to take her by surprise. Whether it was the snap of a twig or a warning call from the crows or possibly just a sixth sense, Alma Goff knew when company was about, and came to stand at the door of her cabin, her narrow ankles ending in worn slippers that made their own soft music as she walked.

She squinted hard at Ellen as she always did, and then her face stretched into a wide smile, the wrinkles folding back upon themselves like old leather. At the temples, her pale skin was paper-thin, exposing the blue veins beneath.

"Knowed you was comin'," she said, opening the torn screen, and Ellen followed her to the kitchen where a pan of water was already simmering.

"Spring water," she said, taking the sassafras from Ellen's hand and dropping it in the pot. "Where the sweet gum grows. Sweet gum makes it sweet."

"*How* did you know I was coming?" Ellen asked, curious.

"Heard a night cry t'other evening, and the first person I thought about after was you."

Ellen watched her stir the tea. "What's a night cry?"

Granny Bo gave her a sidelong look of reproach, as though anybody raised in these hills ought to know. "It's a human sound not made by any human, and the first person you think of after you hear it, that's the person you ought to fix on."

"What's the sound like?"

With fingers thin as sticks, knobby at the joints, Granny Bo reached slowly up to the shelf and clutched two chipped cups which she set on the oilcloth table.

"Can be anything at all—a laugh, a sobbing, a shout. . . ."

"And what was this?"

The small woman pursed her lips. "A cry, I'd say. Like a body crying out."

"But what *is* it?"

Granny Bo shook her head. "Never asked. Some things wasn't meant for us to know. Was a little gal over near Beulah one day wanted to learn about the witch-ing powers, and someone told her to go up on the ridge and set herself down on a log and she was to put one hand under her foot and the other on top of her head and say, 'All the rest belongs to the devil.' And I guess she did, because when they found her she was sittin' that way, with her hand on her foot just so, turned to stone. Died and froze in that position."

The reddish liquid was poured into the cups, and Ellen held the tea to her face, the steam bathing her eyelids. She set her cup back on the table and watched the old woman through the mist.

"You talk like that, Granny, and I'll be afraid to go home."

"There's things worth bein' afraid of and things that aren't," Granny Bo said, and reached for the blueberry bread.

"Dad's got him a selling job now," Ellen told her. "He's a regional representative for the Acme Calendar Company. Be doing some traveling all around the state. Gets a commission every time he takes an order."

"Good for him and bad for you," pronounced Granny Bo.

"Why is that?"

"Get himself a wife drivin' around, goin' places. Man wasn't meant to live unmarried. The good Lord sent me three husbands, but I buried every one of 'em."

Ellen listened politely.

"There's no good in leavin' you home by yourself, though. All *kinds* of things roamin' up here in these hills."

"*What* kinds of things?" Ellen insisted.

"Haints," Granny Bo said.

"Don't seem to scare you any."

"I keep to myself. The ghosts come by here, I mind my own business. But you—you've always got a question in your mouth."

Ellen laughed out loud. "I see any haunts, I'll keep my mouth shut. How's that?"

But the old woman did not laugh, and turned the talk to other things.

When the sun came slanting in the back window, Ellen rose to go:

"You're taking the medicine Dr. George gave you for the dizzy spells?"

"Yep."

"Toothache better?"

"Tooth come out. That was the end of it."

"Well, I'll be back in a few days, then. Would have brought you an egg, but only the leghorn's laying. Don't know what's got into the other hen lately."

"It's the devil," Granny Bo said, going with her to the door. "He come out of old man Keat and went in your horse, and now he's spooked the hen as well."

Turbo got up and stretched as Ellen stepped out. A small bundle of ash twigs, nailed to the doorframe like a charm, caught Ellen's hair as she passed, and she stopped to disentangle herself.

"There's an evilness up here in the backwoods," Granny Bo told her. "Always has been. Comes for a spell and then gives us a rest, but I lived here long enough I know when it's about. Folks say, 'Old Granny Bo and her stories!' but I just go on humming to myself. *I* know."

Ellen felt cold, though it had been warm when she arrived.

"Maybe so," she said. "Take care now."

She could feel the old woman's eyes on her as she started up the trail. Turbo went ahead at a run, tail wagging, glad to be going home.

That night just after ten, as Ellen lay on top her covers, she heard a cry somewhere out in the woods. She raised up on one elbow and listened, and the cry came again.

Only a catbird, she told herself, though that was unlikely at this hour.

A mockingbird making a cat call, she decided, but it was some time before she slept.

Three

"NOW THIS HERE ONE, this is my favorite," Joe Stump said, reaching into his sample case.

Ellen watched expectantly while he drew out a big white square. Already a dozen or more calendars of various sizes stood propped against the wall: calendars with pictures of mountains and the dates printed in blue; calendars with pictures of kittens—a cat for each month—the dates printed in red; calendars with drawings of vegetables and recipes on the other side.

Joe flicked the new calendar around with a flourish. There was a photograph of the Yazoo River at Vicksburg with a steamboat in the background.

"Look," he said, turning the pages. "A different

city on every one of 'em, and all of 'em on the Yazoo. I can start out at Vicksburg and follow the river right up to Tennessee. I'll stop at every town on the calendar and walk in their best hotel. 'How would you like to have a calendar with a picture of your town on it?' I'll ask the manager, 'A calendar in every room?'"

"It's real nice," said Ellen.

"You bet it's nice! And after I sell some to the biggest hotel, I'll stop in at the little ones and say, 'How would you like to have the same kind of calendars the Hotel Majestic has got?'" He winked. "Don't think they won't be begging for them then."

He propped the calendar along the wall with the rest.

"Or I'll walk in Fred's Bait and Tackle and say, 'Fred, how you going to say "Merry Christmas" to all your favorite customers? How about giving each one this here little calendar with space at the bottom to print "Season's Greetings from Fred's Bait and Tackle"?'"

Joe stopped for breath. "'Course, now, if you want something fancy. . . ." He reached for a plastic calendar on a stand with numbers on a movable cylinder. "This here's the Acme's Eternal Calendar, because you can set the numbers to match the month of any year. Never have to throw it away. This is good for banks and funeral parlors, where the word 'eternal' is important. Right at the top, see, that's where the words go . . . 'First National Bank of Tupelo' or something—in gold letters."

"I never knew there were so many kinds of calendars in the whole world," said Ellen.

Her father chuckled. "Well, hang onto your seat,

honey, there's one more to go. I don't know what your mother would have said about this one, but I got to sell to bars and bowling alleys, too."

He pulled out the largest calendar of all. It showed a beautiful young woman in a pair of shorts sitting on an overturned flowerpot. Her legs, held primly together, ended in high-heeled shoes with bows at the ankles. A spade and several packets of seeds were there on the ground, and she was kissing a huge angora cat, which she held in front of her because she wasn't wearing a thing on top.

Ellen studied it. "Any more like this in the fall line, Dad?"

Her father looked embarrassed. "This is about the worst. What do you think?"

"I think she's going to have a hard time working her garden in those high-heeled shoes," said Ellen, and they both laughed.

Joe began putting his calendars back in the sample case. "I just might take to this kind of work," he said. "They say you either have the salesman in you or you don't, and only way to find out is to go the rounds. Already got me an order this morning from the paint store in Millville."

Ellen helped slip the plastic covers over the calendars again. "Places like Vicksburg are a long way off, though, Dad. You going to be on the road a whole lot?"

"Just long enough to make my quota, honey. Man doesn't make his quota, they start lookin' for someone else. Maybe I can sell enough in these parts I won't have to travel much."

Ellen doubted that—not up here in the foothills. But she enjoyed seeing her father get outside himself, go to places he'd never been, talk to people. . . . She wouldn't hold him back.

Joe brought the worry up himself, however. "Only thing bothers me is you here by yourself, Ellen."

"Why? What could happen?"

"Whatever you don't figure on, that's what happens."

"I've got Turbo."

"That's the one thing puts my mind to rest. You keep him in here every night when I'm gone now, hear?"

"I will," Ellen promised. "I won't turn out the light until Turbo's in."

She sat at the open window while her father made out his sales report. He jiggled his knee up and down as he wrote, and every now and then made a whistling noise through his teeth. How many other jobs had there been? Ellen wondered: truck farmer, bricklayer, painter, gas station attendant. . . . There was always enough money for necessities, but a job never lasted more than a few years at the most before Joe was restless to try something else. *Some men are like that,* Mother had told Ellen once. *As long as he's happy and there's food on the table, I don't care.* Ellen didn't either, but she did wonder sometimes if he was happy. Maybe the fact that he had lived up here on Crow's Point all his life made him restless in other ways. Ellen could understand that.

The dusk was heavy with the scent of heliotrope and verbena. Beyond the window the pale white limbs of the sycamore showed up starkly against a forest of cucumber trees. The cicadas chorused, hushed, and chorused again.

A cry came from somewhere just beyond the screen, the same cry Ellen had heard a few nights before. She leaned on the sill, cupping her hands around her eyes, and looked out. There, on the roof of the shed, was a mockingbird, sounding almost like a baby. She had been right. Only a bird. If there were any other kinds of night cries about, only Granny Bo had ears to hear them.

❦

She was flanked by honey locusts, a long uneven line on either side of the lane, beginning at the garden and ending out by the dirt road. They grew in twos and threes, and the spaces between were filled with althea and crape myrtle and privet gone to trees. These in turn were so webbed with vine that even Turbo could not penetrate.

Now and then there would be a space about eye-level, perhaps the size of a small window, where Ellen could see into the pasture on her right. But it afforded only a momentary glance, and the view was swallowed up once again in honeysuckle and kudzu.

She turned her ankle stepping in a rut and stopped to massage it. The holes were as deep as water buckets in some places. Joe Stump had learned to maneuver around them, but he was one of the few drivers who dared.

Whenever Ellen went for the mail, she knew that somewhere, on the other side of the honeysuckle, the dark horse was following. She could smell his horse scent, hear him paw the ground. On this particular morning when she reached a small opening in the foliage, she saw him there on the other side, and her skin prickled. He stood as still as a granite statue at the sight of her, and then, when she moved on, followed her only with his eye. She could hear the red hen clucking and knew that she was there with the horse, the two of them shadowing her like conspirators.

Ellen went ahead hurriedly, concentrating on the distance she had yet to go, calling Turbo to stay by her, like a charm to ward off evil. When Jimmy-Clyde made his deliveries, he brought the mail in as he came, weaving back and forth from one side of the lane to the other, crisscrossing the ruts. The rest of the time, Ellen went for it herself.

She wondered what it would be like when she went to high school in September—whether there would be new friends who would want to come by. How did she tell them that first you took Old Ridge Road up the hillside as far as the small Baptist church and then you turned to the left past the spring. When you got to the place where the creek had washed the road away, you bore to the right, past Gacy's Grocery, to a dirt road without a sign that some called Crow's Point, and you followed it on up past the sweet gum till you came to a mailbox marked "Stump."

How did she go about telling them that she'd be waiting out there by the box, because they might blow a tire coming in—that in the spring rains, in fact, you didn't even take Crow's Point Road—that Ellen would have to walk the five miles down to the junction?

The flag was up on the box, and Ellen opened it to find an ad for termite inspection and the fall catalogue from Sears. She studied the model there on the cover, dressed in a copper-colored suit. Girls like that probably had six or seven pairs of shoes, Ellen thought, one for every outfit they owned.

She tucked the catalogue under her arm and turned back toward the house, stopping to wait for Turbo, who would have preferred going on.

"When the catalogue comes, you order yourself some things," her father had told her the week before. "I don't want my daughter going off to high school looking like she's somebody's no-count, leftover stepchild."

Ellen remembered that awful first day of school last year when she had walked into the classroom wearing a brand new dress with little blue and yellow flowers on it—just right, she had thought, for a warm first day of school. At lunchtime, Beth Larkin, her almost-best-friend, confided—not unkindly—"It's pretty, Ellen, but it looks sort of like a housedress."

All afternoon Ellen's face had burned. She had cringed at every rustle of the starched skirt, at the long row of buttons down the front, from neckline to hem, and the big pockets on either side that she had thought so handy. Clothes, for Ellen, had just been something to put on to stay decent.

As soon as she had reached home that afternoon, she had rushed into the house to look up the dress again in the catalogue, and there it was, under "Easy Care Day Dresses." She hadn't known.

Today, when the *News at Noon* program came on, Ellen sat transfixed as Maureen Sinclair reported on events in Ireland and Israel and some places Ellen had never even heard of. Maureen Sinclair, she was sure, would never make the mistake of buying an easy-care day dress with pockets.

❦❦❦

The phone rang later that afternoon, and Ellen waited before answering: one long ring and one short. That was hers.

"Hello?"

"Ellen?" said Beth Larkin. "You want to come by this afternoon and stay over? My dad could drive out and pick you up."

This time Ellen had an excuse. "Probably can't," she told Beth. "Dad's getting ready for a selling trip next Monday, and I've got to do his shirts."

"Ellen, I swear, you're the hardest girl in the world to get to come over. You're not going to be there alone, are you?"

The question stirred up the uneasiness again that had settled in the pit of Ellen's stomach.

"He'll only be gone three days. Back before I know it," she said, with forced confidence. She heard music in the background that she knew was not coming from Beth Larkin's. Beth heard it too.

"Listen, is somebody else on this line?" Beth asked.

"Sure sounds like it," said Ellen.

"Who do you suppose it is, Ellen?" Beth's voice took on a sarcastic sweetness. "Isn't it a shame that some people don't have anything more to do than listen in on other people's conversations?"

The music cut off.

"Thank you, Mrs. Conklin," Beth said. Ellen laughed.

"Maybe it wasn't Mrs. Conklin," she said. "Maybe it was Grace Talbot."

"It was Mrs. Conklin," Beth said. "That was the theme song for *General Hospital* and Grace Talbot watches *Guiding Light*."

"Well, anyway, Beth—some other time," Ellen told her.

Beth sighed. "That's what you always say."

In a way Ellen wished she had said yes. *Could* have said yes. She liked Beth Larkin—more than anyone else in her class—yet she felt uncomfortable in other people's homes. She and Billy used to talk about staying here forever, picking figs off the trees in summer and pecans off the ground in the fall, but Ellen wondered if it was because they loved Crow's Point so much or because they felt out of place anywhere else.

"You're a loner, just like me," Ellen's mother told her once, and it had seemed a compliment to her independence. Ellen had never been afraid to be lonely before, and she wasn't afraid of it now. But sometimes she felt she said "no" by habit, not by choice.

She looked around her, at all that needed to be done in the kitchen, and knew there was more than enough to occupy her while her father was gone. Ellen squinted, imagining the room growing darker as evening fell and her in the house by herself.

She stood up abruptly, shook her head to rid it of fantasies, and left the room.

Four

THEY WALKED up to the chinaberry tree on
Sunday morning, Ellen and her father, carrying a bou-
quet of red salvia, which grew in a clump by the steps.
Joe always wore a white shirt on Sundays, even though
they never went anywhere but up the hill.

"Smells of rain," he said, his forearms brown beneath the rolled-up sleeves of his shirt. "Good for the
garden if we can get us a steady shower."

Ellen swept up the long brown hair from the nape
of her neck and fixed it to the top of her head with her
mother's bone comb. "We get any steady kind of rain,
you'll float out the driveway and never get back in," she
reminded him.

Joe smiled at her fondly. "I'll get back home
Wednesday if I have to park all the way down in Millville and walk up. Wednesday afternoon, girl, you can
cook the peas and sausage, 'cause I'll be sittin' at the
table come six."

She smiled back at him. "I'll make you a cobbler if
I find enough berries."

There was a breeze that grew stronger the higher
they went. They turned off the path at the fork and
made their way around the bluff toward the gravesites.

Ellen frowned at the weeds that crowded in against her legs. Weeds made it look as though nobody cared.

"Was she sick a long time?" Ellen asked, chagrined that she couldn't remember. "Seemed to me Mom was okay one week and died the next."

"That's about how it was, too," Joe said, plodding along beside her. "It was spinal meningitis. You knew that, didn't you? Wouldn't let me call the doctor. 'A cold's settled in my neck, that's all,' Opal said. 'It'll work itself out.' Then she got to the place where her whole body seemed bent back, and I sent for Dr. George. By the time he got her to the hospital, it was too late."

The yellow balls from the chinaberry tree lay scattered all over the ground, and Ellen crunched them underfoot. The two graves, her mother's and Billy's, lay side by side, with a rosebush in between. The yellow roses bobbed gently, caught up in the morning wind. The quartz stone at the head of her mother's grave picked up the light and shone dusty pink through the clear places.

Turbo fell behind and whined.

"It's all right," said Ellen, holding out her hand to him, but the dog lay down on his belly and put his head on his paws.

Ellen and her father set to work pulling weeds around the rosebush, straightening the stones from Mother's rock garden that Ellen had so patiently carried up the hill, one by one, to make a border around both graves. When they were through, they sat together beneath the chinaberry and savored the breeze on their faces.

"Figure she knows we're here?" Ellen asked.

"That I couldn't speculate on," Joe told her.

Somewhere up in the branches came the three notes of the mourning dove's call. Ellen leaned back against the tree trunk. "I tried to get in touch with Billy once," she said, waiting to see if her father would laugh, but he didn't. "I came here a month after he died, as close to the exact minute and hour as I could, and I said, 'Billy, if your spirit's here, give me a sign.' " She waited again.

"What kind of sign were you figuring on, Ellen April?"

"I don't know. The wind to blow or leaves to fall or a mist to rise or something. Someone told me once that the dead could speak, but nothing happened."

Her father smiled. "And if a seed had dropped from the chinaberry just then and hit you on the head, you would have come a runnin' back home sayin' that you heard from Billy."

"I suppose." Ellen smiled, too.

Joe shook his head. "Reason folks go making up stories is they don't feel easy not having answers. Never could figure why they did that, myself—why they couldn't just say they didn't know and then shut up about it."

Turbo crawled over on his belly until he was close to Ellen's feet and lay there. Whenever she moved, he perked up his ears, eager to be going.

"Funny thing, though," Ellen's father went on. "Granny Bo predicted Opal's death."

Ellen felt her head turning as if some unseen power had hold of it. "What?"

"Something she said once—almost a month before Opal took sick. I'd taken her some of Opal's soup, and she asked if I could cook for myself. I told her not much to speak of—joking with her, you know, the way I do—and she looks at me and says, 'Could be you'll end up a widower, Joe Stump, and you ought to learn to make do.'"

"Could have been a passing remark," said Ellen.

"Could have. But I says to the old granny, 'What makes you think I might?' and she says, 'I see things coming I don't like to see, but I sees them anyway.' Well, I didn't pay it hardly any mind at all till Opal took sick, and when she died, it was as though Granny Bo was right there in the room with me, holding onto my arm. Not the first thing she's predicted that's come true."

"Then you *do* believe her?"

"All I'm saying is I don't understand, one way or the other. To believe in Granny Bo's predictions, you'd have to keep track how many times she's right and how many times she's wrong before it meant anything. Folks always remember the ones that come true, and it gets all out of proportion." He stood up to go, and Turbo leaped to his feet, tail wagging.

"Granny Bo told me the other day that there's an evilness here in these woods," Ellen said.

Joe put his arm around his daughter's shoulder as they headed back down to the house. "There's always evilness about—up here, down in Millville, over in Merwyn City. . . . Doesn't matter where you go, you got to look out for it. Nothing new about that. What you got to learn is when to doubt and when to trust, and that's not something that comes easy."

The extra pair of pressed trousers went in the bottom of the old suitcase, the underwear next, and the two freshly laundered shirts—one for each day—lay on top. Ellen checked them all again before she snapped the lid shut.

"Well, well, look at me!" Joe Stump said, smiling at his reflection in the mirror. From behind, the seat of his trousers was shiny, but Ellen hoped it wouldn't matter. Seen from the front, he could have been an insurance man or a preacher, even.

"Wouldn't your mother have liked to see me all dressed up like this? Never thought I'd have me a job have to put on a clean shirt every day," said Joe.

Ellen tucked the carefully folded handkerchief in his vest pocket so that the points showed just above the top.

"You've got to look nice now, Dad," she said. "Don't want you walking in any Hotel Majestic looking like a no-count, leftover stepfather."

They laughed.

He glanced at his watch. "Well, if I start out now I should be in Starkville by noon, time enough to see the man at the hardware store and drive on to Greenwood. You take care now, honey, and if anything makes you uneasy, you call Dwight Ruggles."

"Sure," said Ellen, knowing she wouldn't. The one time there had been excitement in the backwoods, the one time robbers rode through, it was Dwight Ruggles who found them on Old Ridge Road with a flat tire and helped them change it. Didn't know who they were till they got away. The reason Dwight Ruggles was sheriff was that no one else wanted the job. But to Joe's way of thinking, at least the man wore a badge, and that must count for something.

Ellen stood out on the porch and watched her father drive off, glad she had packed some rolls and ham for his lunch. She tried to imagine him sleeping all night in his car and still looking fresh the next morning.

"I'm the only man in the world can sleep just as good sitting up as lying down," Joe had told her, when she chided him for not getting a motel.

The car was out of sight behind the honey locusts and crape myrtle, but Ellen waited until she heard it turn onto Crow's Point Road before she went inside. The sassafras tree near the porch seemed to rustle as she passed.

It was the first time in her life that she would be alone overnight, Ellen realized. She kept busy, though, and whenever she felt even a quiver of anxiety, shoved it back out of consciousness. By the time *News at Noon* came on, she was secure in her old routine and had made a list of all she planned to do in the next three days. Paint the cupboards, for one. Order her clothes from Sears. Make plum jelly.

She worked steadily all afternoon and into the evening and treated herself to a supper of cold cornbread and huckleberries with cream. She would never have gotten away with serving a meal like this to her father. Maybe it would be an adventure—having him gone.

About eight o'clock, after she had bathed, she wrapped a towel around her hair and went to sit on the porch as fireflies rose up from the tall grass along the edge of the lane.

There was a low growl from somewhere out in the yard, and Ellen strained to see through the dusk.

"Turbo?" she said.

The dog was standing just beyond the rock garden, ears laid back, tail straight, facing the bluff. He did not turn when she called him, but growled again.

"What is it, boy?" Ellen asked, going out to him. She could see nothing. Nothing at all. Still the dog stood, however, the hair raised along the ridge of his spine, his nose pointed in the direction of the chinaberry. At last Ellen took him by the collar and pulled him inside, latching the screen behind her.

There was something about the way the hills faced each other that made sounds carry. Ellen had always known that. When she was small and the Brodys lived in the neighboring house, she used to be awakened sometimes by the slam of a car door, even though it was on the other side of the bluff. There were even times Ellen imagined she could hear a distant noise from Granny Bo's—the braying of her old mule or a hammering on the porch.

She thought of all this the following day as she set about painting the kitchen cupboards. She had seen nothing, heard nothing, when Turbo growled. It could have been a scent. A weasel, perhaps.

She called in her grocery order to Gacy's and was disappointed when Irene answered instead of her jovial mother.

"Margarine's gone up," Irene interrupted sourly as Ellen read off her list.

If it were Mrs. Gacy on the line, she would have

commented first on the weather and asked about Ellen's health and even inquired about how Granny Bo was doing. But Irene Gacy, fortyish and single, had never cared much for her life at the junction and showed it.

"Saw your dad drive by yesterday in a suit and tie," Irene said, after Ellen had finished. "'Joe Stump's either going to a wedding or a funeral,' I told Mother." She paused, waiting for Ellen to fill in the details.

For a moment Ellen toyed with the idea of saying that her father was courting a widow down in Millville, just so Irene Gacy would have something to spread around, but then she thought better of it.

"He got himself a job with the Acme Calendar Company," Ellen told her. "Doing some traveling, that's all."

"And leaving *you* up there alone?"

The question again. It was composed of words with sharp edges that made Ellen suck in her breath. The more she was asked it, the more determined she became.

"I've got Turbo, and we're doing just fine," she said.

Around noon there was the rattle of a bicycle on the lane, the familiar "Hi," and then Jimmy-Clyde walked in the open hallway, stopping at the kitchen door with a sack of groceries.

"Jimmy-Clyde," said Ellen. "I could just about set my watch by you."

He looked at her uncertainly. "I'm not very late."

"Of course you're not. Right on time as usual."

He beamed and began the ritual removing of each item from the sack, his tongue between his lips after each pronouncement: "Heinz catsup; Ajax; soap;

orange juice; eggs. . . ." He put the carton on the table and looked at it quizzically. "I thought you had some chickens."

"We do, but only one's laying."

"No use having chickens if you don't get any eggs," said Jimmy-Clyde.

"Exactly."

The recitation went on: "Baking soda, margarine and blackstrap molasses." He set the bottle on the table with a thunk. "That's what Granny Bo bought when she came in. Blackstrap molasses."

"It makes good gingerbread," Ellen said.

"A big jug of it," Jimmy-Clyde continued. "Irene says she uses it to make spells."

"Irene Gacy's got a mouth as big as a well. Her mother ought to put a cover on it," said Ellen, putting the things away.

"What's spells?" Jimmy-Clyde asked.

Ellen turned and looked at him. Every so often his innocence startled her. "It's what people talk about when they can't explain something," she said, and then, realizing that Jimmy-Clyde couldn't possibly understand, added, "Spells are nonsense, that's what."

"Oh," said Jimmy-Clyde.

After he had gone out to take care of the horse, Ellen dipped her brush in the paint again, thinking of Granny Bo. Just what kind of spells was she supposed to make with blackstrap molasses? It wasn't the first time Ellen had heard such stories, of course, and whenever the old woman shopped at Gacy's she managed to do something to make people talk—Irene, anyway.

Ellen heard the clunk of the shovel finally against

the barn as Jimmy-Clyde finished his work, and then he came in the kitchen with a smile so wide that his face seemed too small to contain it.

"Know what I found?" he said, holding out his hands, one cupped over the other. He lifted the top one reverently. An egg nestled in the palm of his pudgy hand.

"The red hen lays in Sleet's stall just to spite me," Ellen said, taking the egg. "Thanks, Jimmy-Clyde. Here—let me pay you for last week."

Jimmy-Clyde pedaled away happy.

About four o'clock, as Ellen was cleaning her paint brush, she saw Turbo sit up, ears bent forward.

"What is it, boy?" Ellen asked. She fanned herself with the flaps of the old shirt she was wearing.

The dog got up and moved slowly toward the door, then out into the open hallway. He stood stone still for a moment, then—paw after paw—crept onto the porch, body low, ears laid back, tail taut. Ellen followed.

She stood in the breezeway, straining to hear what the dog was hearing.

"What on earth *is* it, Turbo?" she asked again.

A low growl came from the dog's throat, stopped, and began again. Ellen stared out over the pasture. She saw only the dark horse standing against the fence, staring back.

Five

SHE WENT to Granny Bo's the next day carrying nothing but a question. Up the trail to the bluff, down the other side, into the woods where the ginseng grew, and then the long raggedy path that led hill over hill to the cabin with its heaped-up vine-covered roof. The brown mule, its quivery ears purple-looking, studied her from behind the shed.

They sat on Granny's porch this time, facing each other—Ellen sideways on the steps, Granny on the rusted metal glider. The old woman wore a faded apron, pinned to her dress at the shoulder. Every inch of her face was covered with wrinkles, and at the outer corner of each eye, the skin drooped down like a curtain. She rocked steadily, pushing against the floor with her old gray slippers, her stockings rolled just below the knees.

Ellen asked her question:

"If the devil's in Sleet, how do I get rid of it?" Even asking, her mouth felt dry. To ask was to believe.

Granny Bo's knobby fingers twitched in her lap, then grew still. Her gums moved up and down a time or two before she spoke: "Thing about the devil is you don't get rid of 'im."

"What do you do?" Ellen struggled to keep her distance, yet the question itself betrayed her.

"Got to git 'im out of the horse and into somethin' else," Granny Bo said finally.

Crows were cawing from the trees overhead, preparing one last foray before dark. Ellen watched the old woman's eyes squint until they were little slits under her thick white eyebrows. "How do you do that?" she asked.

"That's the ugliness of it," Granny replied. "Not a thing in this world you can do, 'cause the devil don't need no help. Sometimes—like when a person dies—the devil will come right out and go into whatever's handy. That's what happened to your horse, I'm thinking. When a body *don't* die, though, the devil stays there till somebody meaner comes along, and then he jumps on his back."

Ellen was struck by the humor of it and was instantly reassured. It was beginning to sound like the folk tales they had read back in fourth grade.

"Do you really believe all this?" she asked, smiling.

Granny Bo studied her intently, and Ellen was sorry she had smiled. "See that ash tree out there in the yard?" the old woman said, pointing. "Don't make no difference whether I believe in it or not; it's there."

Ellen's uneasiness returned. She dropped her eyes and concentrated on a pair of flickers taking a dust bath in the bare dirt yard.

"Same with my youngest," Granny Bo went on. "All the signs pointed to the devil in 'im, and I just didn't pay it no heed. Paid it no mind at all. I didn't *want* to know, you see. Ever' where that boy went there was trouble, and I was too thick to see it. Raised me four other children and I figured the fifth would be the same. But it's the fifth, they say, the devil takes, he can't get his claws on somethin' else."

Ellen tried to imagine Alma Goff with children. That was long before Ellen's time. Ever since she'd known the old woman, it had just been Granny Bo, here in the cabin alone.

"What happened to your children?" Ellen asked after a moment.

"First three was girls, and they're married. Scattered all over the country, they are. Oldest boy, he's down in Hattiesburg."

Ellen waited. "And the fifth . . . ?" she asked finally.

Granny Bo's hands twitched again, then dropped to the glider cushion and pushed till she was on her feet. "Died," she said, without expression, and started for the door. "Gone off and died. Come on back in the kitchen, Ellen, and we'll have us a biscuit."

It was easy to see how Granny Bo and her "powers" made talk, Ellen thought, as she watched her unwrap a small package of biscuits and pour the tea. The room was dark, with only one window on the north to light it, and the dusty shelves were lined with dark bags of this and that, and bunches of dry herbs. There were no colored plates, no fancy cups, no decorated pitchers that other women kept in their kitchens. Two tin cans with dead geraniums sat on the windowsill where green curtains fluttered, their hems worn. Granny Bo was talking spirits again.

"Yes, they's boogers and witches and haints about,

but they's the night cry too, and sometimes that's a blessing."

"What do you mean?" Ellen bit into the biscuit and found it hard as leather. When Granny wasn't looking, she slipped it into the pocket of her jeans to give to Turbo.

"Well, sometimes the night cry's there to he'p you. It's a warning, you might say, that something's afoot."

Ellen thought it over. "Last week, when I was down, you said you'd heard a night cry, and the first person you thought of after was me."

"Hadn't forgot. Didn't mean you were up to somethin'. Just meant that whatever was fixing to happen, you figured in it someways."

Well, that certainly covered all bases, Ellen thought.

"I've got to get on home now," she said, finishing her tea. "Dad'll be back tomorrow, and I got loads to do before then."

"There's a full moon tonight," Granny Bo said, following her to the door. "You take care now, Opal."

It wasn't the first time she had called Ellen by her mother's name. Granny Bo always had said they resembled each other, but as Ellen set off, she wondered about the woman's mind and the way it strayed. Sometimes she was talking about yesterday and sometimes she was talking about tomorrow and sometimes she was talking about twenty years ago as though it had just happened that morning. Time, to an old woman, got all scrambled somehow, and when she tried to put the pieces together, she got them in the wrong place. Her youngest son, for example, could have died when he was three or thirteen or thirty, and it would always be like yesterday to a mother who undoubtedly missed him, devil or not.

Down the first hill and up the next. It was a long way home, and Ellen wished she had started sooner. The sun had set and everything around her had a gray look. A half hour passed before she reached the place where the ginseng grew.

It was there the horse had bolted. Somewhere there in the shadows was the very rock against which Billy had bashed his head. Ellen had thought more than once of unearthing it and sending it plunging down the hillside, but she would not stop to do it now. When Turbo tarried in the underbrush, she lured him on with the biscuit and was glad when the bluff was in sight at last.

At the top, however, the dog stopped abruptly, ears cocked, tail stiff. But Ellen was in no mood to dawdle.

"*Come,* Turbo," she said sharply, and they started down the other side toward the clearing.

It was good to be home again. Ellen turned on the lamp in the parlor, and the yellow pine-board walls gave off a welcoming glow. The light brought out the colors in the rag rug and illuminated the photo of Ellen's mother there on the mantel. The hearth and chimney were of slate, taken from the hills, and seemed to make the room one with the land beyond.

Ellen got out the sewing basket and tackled the holes in the heels of her father's socks, using the darning needle. Back and forth, threads going crosswise, the way her mother had taught her, then up and down, weaving the threads over and under the others until they made a tightly woven patch. Strangely, she had not particularly minded the first night alone, but she minded this one. Moths threw themselves against the screen, flew off, then hurled themselves once more.

What could possibly happen? she had asked her father, and he had answered, *Whatever you don't figure on, that's what happens.* She got up and bolted the door. She did not relish bedtime, when she had to cross the open hallway to get to the rooms on the other side.

"We ought to close that breezeway," her mother had said once, a long time ago. "They don't make houses like this anymore, Joe. Be awful nice to walk from the bedroom to the kitchen of a December morning without freezing yourself."

And Ellen's father had said, "I'll close it when I can get around to it, Opal." But of course he never did.

Ellen's mother had not spoken to him sharply, nor he to her. It was an interaction Ellen had grown comfortable with over the years—her mother's reminders of things to be done and her father's acknowledgments, and meanwhile life went on as it always had and nothing got done and no one got upset.

Ellen thought she heard a noise out in the barn and held her breath, listening intently. But Turbo, on the floor beside her, slept on. She picked up the next sock to be darned.

She thought again of her mother. Opal had been young when she married—only seventeen—and Ellen was born a year later. It was Mother who, on the first warm day of spring, would take off her shoes and wade in the creek near the back of the pasture, squealing delightedly at the mud that oozed up between her toes. It was Mother who swung highest of all in the swing

Father had hung for them in the beech tree. "Higher," she would shriek to Joe, who pushed from behind, and with each forward thrust, her laughter rang out over the clearing. Up here on the Stumps's own land, Opal had seemed thoroughly at home; but beyond Crow's Point, she was as shy and uncertain as a schoolgirl and had passed it on to Ellen like an inheritance.

The noise came again—the unmistakable sound of the barn door closing, the familiar squeak of the hinge that Ellen had known all her life. She leaped up, her throat dry, letting the darning slide to the floor. Turbo jerked himself awake, a low growl coming from his throat.

Ellen was certain that the barn door had been bolted before she came in. She always made *sure* that it was, so that Sleet could not get out and come near the house.

She moved over to check the latch on the parlor door, knowing all the time just how senseless it was to do it. There wasn't a window screen in the house that couldn't be pushed through. Ellen leaned against the wall, hugging herself with her arms, while Turbo went into a frenzy of barking. If she could turn out the light, she thought, she might be able to see what was out there. She began to inch her way back to the lamp, dragging Turbo along beside her.

Ellen was within three feet of the lamp when she heard soft thudding sounds just outside the window. Whether footsteps or horse's hooves, she could not tell, but panic overwhelmed her.

"Turbo, stay with me. Help me," Ellen whispered, sinking down to her knees, one arm around the dog's neck.

Then, slowly, she edged toward the light and, with shaking fingers, reached out and turned the switch. The lamp went off, and the thudding outside stopped abruptly. Moonlight streamed through the window.

Turbo was beside himself, alternately yelping and growling. Ellen stood up slowly, still clutching his collar, and started on across the room toward the phone in the kitchen. But whom would she call? Dwight Ruggles? Even if she found the sheriff home, it would take a half hour for him to drive up from Millville.

As she neared the side window, Ellen could see the barn silhouetted against the web of clouds, the outline of the beech tree, the shed. And then, so close she had not even noticed, the figure of a man, just a few feet from the sill.

Six

TERROR SHOT through her, exploding in her chest.

Turbo rose up on his hind legs, front paws on the sill, barking in spasms, his body shaking.

The man backed off.

"Hello?"

Ellen did not move, holding her breath as though the mere sound of it would give her away. The figure outside seemed to her half-man, half-devil as the shoulders hunched up in the moonlight.

"Hello?" the man called again. He did not come closer. "Listen, I need help."

Hidden in the darkness of the house, Ellen knew she had the advantage. She would not get rid of him by silence, however.

"I open this door, mister, the dog will take your arm off," she called out.

The man raised his hands as if in surrender. "I won't come any closer."

"You tell me your business, and then you get out of here," Ellen called.

"I need some food for myself and a sick wife."

"Where's your wife?"

The stranger jerked his head in the direction of the bluff. "We're staying in that old house the other side of the ridge. Moving on in a few days." He lowered his hands cautiously and let them hang loosely. "Should have come right to your door, I guess. Thought I might find something out in the barn without troubling you folks for it—eggs, maybe."

"That was a mistake, all right," Ellen answered. "We don't like folks prowling around, not bold enough to come to the door and ask."

"Well, I'm asking now," the man replied.

Ellen thought it over. Still her heart pounded.

"I tell you what, mister, you sit down on the log out there where we can keep an eye on you and don't you move. I'll get some things together and put them on the porch."

"I mean to work for it," the man said. "I'm not asking charity."

"You were right willing to steal for it."

"Well, I mean to make amends. I can chop wood, cut hay—whatever you got."

"Best you take the food and go," Ellen said. "You stay put, or I'll set the dog on you."

The man sat down and waited. Ellen moved quickly into the kitchen where she could watch him from that window. Every few seconds she glanced out, but the stranger had not moved. Turbo continued barking from his post in the other room.

Ellen left the door of the refrigerator open and worked by its light, not wanting to let the man catch a glimpse of her, know her age. Hurriedly she put together some cold baked beans, the last of the ham, some cheese, plums, and a mayonnaise jar full of milk. She placed them in a sack and then, checking once more out the window, unlatched the door. Holding onto Turbo with one hand, she moved into the breezeway and set the bag on the porch. Turbo strained at his collar, but she pulled him back inside. The man still sat.

"All right," she called through the side window, after she had latched the door. "There's a sack waiting."

"Thank you," the man said, and slowly stood up, moving toward the porch. He was big-boned, but not heavy, almost as tall as her father. Ellen could make out nothing more. He disappeared around the corner of the house, then passed the front window. Ellen heard him on the steps, the porch, and finally he reappeared in the clearing with the bag in his arms. He gave a kind of salute, and then he was lost in the shadows. She wondered which way he had come—the path up over the ridge or the gate at the back of the pasture.

Her shoulders ached with tension, and she sank

down in the chair, shaking with relief. It could all be a ruse, of course, to catch her off guard. The one man could walk away from the front door, and another could walk in the back. But somehow she felt that the danger, for now, was past. How long had he been in the Brodys' old house? Surely that accounted for Turbo's behavior of the last few days.

She did not turn on the light again. A half-hour later, with Turbo close beside her, Ellen crossed the open hallway to the bedrooms on the other side and latched the door quickly behind her. She lay with the dog at her feet, a flashlight by her pillow. Her ears strained at every noise, deciphering the slightest squeak. But all she heard were the familiar scuttlings of squirrels on the roof and a mockingbird singing from the chimney. If the man had returned, he made no sound.

❦

He was sitting on the log again the next morning when Ellen got up. He had come so silently and sat so still that even Turbo had not known he was out there. Ellen startled when she saw him and drew back from the window, studying him from behind the curtain.

The man had a sand-colored beard and hair badly in need of a trim. Ellen tried to determine his age: about seven or eight years younger than her father, she decided. She felt somewhat reassured that he had come again without bothering her.

Turbo woke and stretched. Immediately he caught the stranger's scent and began to growl.

"Be quiet now," Ellen told him as she washed up at the sink, pulling her long hair back with a rubber band.

When she was dressed, she put a leash on Turbo's collar and went outside. The dog strained toward the man, barking.

"Stay, Turbo," she said.

"Mornin'," the man said, getting up slowly, his eye on Turbo.

"Morning," Ellen said cautiously, and waited.

"I come by to work for the meal you gave me, and lunch too if you can spare it."

"I didn't ask any payment," Ellen told him.

The man motioned toward the ridge again. "Don't want to move on till the wife's better, and I'd be obliged if I could earn us our meals for a few days."

Ellen wondered what she should say.

"I can milk a cow, fix a roof, pluck a chicken. . . ."

"Don't have a cow, and there's only two hens left, so you won't be plucking them," Ellen said, then added, "You just missed my father, but he'll be home again this afternoon. You'd best talk to him."

She wondered if the man knew she was lying— knew, in fact, that she had been here alone all night. She felt his eyes on her and decided he knew.

"Dorothy's going to need some lunch," he said steadily, "but I wouldn't feel right taking it, 'less you give me some work to do."

"Well, there's a garden the other side of the house," Ellen told him. "You can start on that if you like. Hoe's in the barn."

He turned abruptly and crossed the clearing. A few minutes later he was in the garden, back bent, hacking away at the weeds.

Ellen watched him as she made her bed. He did not look quite so menacing as he had the night before, silhouetted against the sky. She was not foolish enough to unleash Turbo, however. He'd sniff at the man for a minute and then rush off to chase a rabbit. She wanted him near.

Once she looked out and saw Sleet standing at the fence by the barn, body taut, staring over at the man in the garden. And then, as she watched, the man straightened, rested his hand on the hoe and, turning slowly, fixed his gaze on the dark horse as though a message had passed between them.

Ellen shrank back against the wall, feeling once more the pounding of blood in her temples. But the familiar surroundings of her own room comforted her, and finally she shrugged off her fears as imaginings only.

By eleven, when the garden was half done and the stranger showed no sign of stopping, Ellen gathered up her courage and went out, Turbo beside her. She tried this time to be pleasant. Cautiously pleasant.

" 'Bout time you stopped for something to eat, isn't it?" she asked.

He wiped one sleeve across his forehead. Beneath the heavy eyebrows his eyes were dark, set far back in his head.

"Guess I might take something to Dorothy."

They walked toward the house together, the stranger keeping his distance.

"Long way to go?" Ellen asked after a moment.

"Got the beets and squash yet to do. Then I'll start on the corn."

"No—I mean with your wife—where you're traveling to."

"I'm taking her down to her sister's in Biloxi," the man answered, without expression.

Ellen's wariness returned. "You sure took a round-about way to go to Biloxi, coming all the way up here."

He made no reply for a moment, then answered, "Had to find me a place to stay over with Dorothy. Sure can't afford a motel."

No, Ellen thought, looking at his worn clothes. *He probably can't.*

She went inside to get the sack, and this time handed it to him herself. Turbo sniffed at the man's shoes and trousers without growling.

The stranger gave his peculiar sort of salute again in thanks, then headed out toward the pasture. "I'll finish the garden after lunch," he called over his shoulder.

Ellen set to work on the cobbler she had promised her father and wondered what she would cook for the man and his wife over the next few days. Better get a turkey from Gacy's the next time she phoned an order in. Could stretch out a turkey for a week if she had to—cook up some black-eyed peas to go with it.

Soon the kitchen was filled with the aroma of wood burning in the stove, mingling with the smell of hot cast iron. It reminded Ellen of a long time ago when her grandmother was alive, polishing the chrome trim. That memory was replaced with her mother's face, her mother's biscuits. Now the kitchen was hers alone, and she wished that just once, when she and Billy used to play at dividing things up, she had let him have the stove. Ellen flicked a drop of water on top of it. She could tell by the way the drop danced that it was time to put the cobbler in.

Music from the TV drifted into the kitchen, and Ellen hummed along. There was a strange kind of comfort in having neighbors again, even the untalkative stranger and his sick wife.

"*News at Noon,* with Maureen Sinclair," the announcer was saying, and Ellen went to the doorway to watch.

The attractive brunette there on the screen wore a dark blouse with thin ribbons of lace at the cuffs. Ellen stood looking down at her own clothes—the jeans she'd worn all summer and the tee shirt with Niagara Falls on the front.

"Good afternoon," Maureen Sinclair said, but her voice sounded all gargling, and before she got any further, the sound went off. Ellen went in and shook the set, but nothing happened.

She plopped disgustedly down in the easy chair and watched the silent picture, trying to guess what Maureen Sinclair was reporting. There was a picture of a plane crash, then of troops marching, and then a funeral— somebody important; it must be in Spain, Ellen thought. Between each sequence, there was Maureen Sinclair, sitting right there in the studio in Merwyn City, but as connected with events in Austria and Russia and Spain as if she had traveled there that very week.

A pause for a commercial, the set silent, and then the local news. There was the main street in Millville, and a shot of the new Robert L. Cory Auditorium. There were pictures of teenagers Ellen didn't know, working on a float, and a baker making a cake and a band practicing a march. Ellen could only guess that the town was getting ready for the dedication of the building the following week. This was followed by a sequence of Robert L. Cory himself and his wife and son, playing croquet on the lawn of their home in California, right on a cliff by the ocean. The house in the background looked like a palace to Ellen. What would it be like for him to come back here? Why on earth would he want to?

The stranger came back about two, took the hoe again from the side of the house, and went right to work, and the afternoon sped by without Ellen even thinking about him.

It was not quite four when Joe Stump's car came winding up the rutted lane. Turbo heard it first and went yelping happily out into the clearing. Ellen waited on the porch. The old Chevy shuddered and stopped, and Joe got out, smiling broadly. He came over and gave Ellen a bear hug, squeezing the bones in her upper arms and rubbing his grizzled cheek next to hers.

"Dog-*gone* but it's good to be back!" he said, and then his eye caught sight of the man beyond in the garden. He paused, letting go of Ellen, and stared.

"Who the devil is that?" he asked.

Seven

ELLEN TOLD the story with a touch of humor—
how she had panicked at the sound of the barn door,
the way she had clung to Turbo, the threat she had
made to turn him loose on the stranger. . . .

But Joe Stump didn't laugh. His brows furrowed
when she told him she had gone outside and left a sack
of food on the porch.

"Could have been a mess of them out there, Ellen
April. You never knowed what you were walking into."

"A mess of them out there, I figured they would
have broken in by then," she answered.

"Figured right this time, maybe, but you may not
the next." Joe set his bag on the steps. "Guess I ought
to go over and be civil, anyways." He studied the man
from a distance. "Looks like someone I ought to know,
but I sure can't place him. He tell you his name?"

"I didn't ask," said Ellen.

She followed him over to the large garden, hemmed
in on three sides by vine. The man turned when he saw
Joe coming. His beard glistened with sweat, his shirt
was soaked through.

"Evenin'," Joe said.

"Evenin'." The man straightened up cautiously,
then shook the hand that Joe extended.

"Joe Stump," Ellen's father said, by way of introduction. "You happen to be one of the Hawkes boys up near the Tennessee line? Seems like I remember you from somewheres."

The man hestitated a moment, then smiled faintly. "There's a whole tribe of us scattered around. Gerald's the name. Gerald Hawkes."

"On your way to Biloxi, Ellen tells me."

The man nodded. "The wife . . ." He stared out over the garden. "Her mind's gone, you see, and I'm turnin' her over to her sister. She's been like this for right some time now, and nothing more I can do for her."

Ellen stared silently at the man, then looked at her father. She saw his eyes soften. "A shame," Joe said. "A crying shame."

Gerald shifted uncomfortably. "If it's all the same to you, I'd appreciate your not tellin' anyone about Dorothy—about our passing through. It's an embarrassment, you know, coming back to your own people with a wife who's not right in the head."

"I understand," Joe said.

Gerald stabbed at the ground with the hoe. "Dorothy's got herself to the place she thinks folks are trying to do her harm. Can hardly keep the car on the road the way she's always grabbin' at my arm, anybody comes our way. Knew there was houses up here, some of 'em empty. Thought I'd stop a bit, nobody around, see if I couldn't quiet her down before we go on. Only come a hundred miles, and that took a whole day."

"Where's home for you now?"

"Small town south of Nashville. We won't be here

long, and I'm not asking favors. I aim to work for what we eat."

"Well, you stay as long as you need to," Joe told him kindly. "Won't be the first folks that made use of the old Brody place."

As Ellen followed her father back to the house, she realized that Gerald must have seen Joe's suitcase there on the front steps. It made a lie of her pretense the night before that there were others in the house beside herself, and that Gerald had just missed her father that morning. But when she turned to see if Gerald was watching, she saw him hard at work again, his back to the house.

"How'd the trip go, Dad?" she asked, as they went inside.

"I made a lot of contacts," Joe told her. "Laid the groundwork, you might say."

It wasn't a good trip, Ellen concluded. But Joe Stump could see a silver lining in a sink hole, Mother used to say, and he was talking silver linings now.

"Got to go back next week and see a man in Vicksburg. Owns a chain of motels, they tell me." He turned to Ellen. "Even thought me up a slogan while I was driving home this afternoon: 'If there's a Gideon in the drawer, there's an Acme on the wall.'"

Ellen looked at him blankly. "What's a Gideon?"

Joe burst out laughing. "Honey, we got to get you out of these hills and down where it's civilized. Gideon's a kind of Bible put in hotel rooms for folks to read. People talk about a Gideon Bible, you know they was in a hotel or motel."

"Oh," said Ellen.

· 61 ·

She began setting the table, and Joe talked to her from across the hall as he unpacked.

"Only got two orders this trip, honey, but we're going to Gacy's tomorrow and buy you some shoes. I'm not sending my daughter to high school with shoes all run down at the heels."

"We've got bigger problems than that, Dad," Ellen told him. "TV's broken. Picture's okay, but the sound's gone. All you get are people opening and closing their mouths like goldfish."

Even from across the hall, Ellen could hear him sigh.

"Well, next week I'll make enough to buy us a color set, Ellen. I can feel it coming. Won't be a town on the Yazoo River don't know Joe Stump was there."

Ellen silently placed a container of applesauce in the bottom of the sack she was packing for Gerald. What was it about her father? she wondered. He was always jumping from one thing to another—his eye on a project that never seemed to work out. But the failures never stopped him, never—as far as Ellen could tell—slowed him down. He was as enthusiastic over each new idea as a kid over Christmas, and listening to him talk now, you'd think it had been his life's ambition to work for Acme. Ellen wondered how long a man could go without getting discouraged, at what point her father—like Gerald about his wife—might just give up.

"It's okay about Gerald Hawkes working here, then?" she asked Joe at dinner.

He buttered a slice of bread and slanted it against the edge of his plate. "Sure ain't going to turn away nobody with a sick wife."

"You knew him once?"

"Knowed one of the Hawkeses, a friend of Dad's. Ison and his two brothers had a whole mess of kids. Never could keep 'em straight. Spread out all over the map by now, I reckon."

Ellen toyed with her peas. "I suppose he'll take Dorothy to Biloxi and go off and leave her."

"Not for us to judge him, Ellen April. Man can take just so much before he breaks," Joe said. "I'm not going to say another word to him about it."

<center>~~~~</center>

The summer rain streamed down the window of Gacy's General Store. As Ellen sat waiting her turn on the bench at the back, surrounded by shoeboxes, she thought of how the lane at home would be mud and they'd have to walk in from the road.

She was also listening to the conversation next to her between a customer and Irene Gacy—the tall, thin daughter of Tom and Nellie Gacy.

"Can't help it," the customer was saying. "Every time there's a full moon, I think of her. 'Trouble comes in threes, and the devil rides in on the third one,' Alma Goff told me once, and the week after that, my boy broke his arm in three places. She's a prophet, that woman, sure as I'm sittin' here."

"Prophet's *one* word for it," humphed Irene, the left side of her mouth sagging. "Not what *I'd* call it, exactly."

"Oh, Irene, now!"

"Seems to me," Irene went on, raising her voice so everyone could hear, . . . "seems to me that when a person can predict the future, she's got a hand in it someways."

"Some of her predictions come true and some don't," Ellen put in quietly. "If you kept a record, my dad says, you'd see it wasn't anything to get excited over."

Irene humphed again. "Trouble is, the predictions that *have* come true were the very worst kind."

"She's just an old woman who's had a lot of sorrow in her life," Ellen defended. "Lost three husbands and a son."

Irene raised her eyebrows.

"I never heard anything about her losing a son," she said curiously. "If Alma Goff's got a dead boy, she's the only one knows where he's buried. And that's against the law—burying your own kin without calling in the coroner."

Ellen's eyes snapped. Irene Gacy could start more gossip indirectly than anybody else in the backwoods.

"Not right in the head," a second customer said, fingering the yard goods. "I remember how Granny Bo used to ride down to Millville on that mule. She'd wander around the streets, stopping any little boy she passed, giving him pennies. . . . My aunt used to say, 'You mark my words, she's going to walk off with somebody's child one of these days.' Never know what that old woman's up to next."

Irene lifted her chin and cast Ellen a triumphant smile.

Ellen got up and left. It was pathetic how important Irene Gacy felt in this little rundown store way up here at the junction when there were women like Maureen Sinclair who knew everything that was going on in the world and didn't act half so uppity.

She went outside, past sweet Mrs. Gacy at the cash

register, who surely deserved a better daughter, and sprinted across the road in the rain. She would order her shoes from Sears and have a lot more styles to choose from.

◆⑤◆

Crow's Point Junction consisted of Gacy's General Store, a gas station, a sprinkling of houses, and Dr. George's home-office. Joe Stump had told Ellen he'd meet her in the waiting room, so Ellen ran up the gravel drive.

It worried her that her father was seeing the doctor. If he was sick, he hadn't mentioned it to Ellen, but of course he never would.

Trouble comes in threes, Old Granny Bo was supposed to have said. Well, what of it? If you waited long enough, you could always find three troubles to lump together . . . *and the devil rides in on the third one.* If her mother's death was trouble number one, and Billy's was number two, her father getting sick would be the worst of all, because that might leave Ellen up here on Crow's Point by herself.

She sucked in her breath, held it, then let it out as she opened the door of the office. There were no other patients waiting, and Ellen reached for a *National Geographic* to pass the time. The door to the examining room had been left open, however, and she could hear her father's voice from inside:

"Now this here one—this is just the thing for a doctor's office, right out there under the clock."

Oh, no! Ellen closed her eyes.

There was the sound of a briefcase unsnapping.

"The Grand Canyon," Joe Stump announced dra-

· 65 ·

matically. "Just the thing to get your patients' minds off their troubles. And right there at the bottom we'll print, 'See your doctor once a year.'"

Ellen covered her face with her hands.

"I'll take it, Joe." Dr. George laughed. "Probably the closest this man will ever get to the Grand Canyon."

"And when folks ask where you got it," Joe said, "you tell 'em the Acme Calendar Company's got a representative right up here in Crow's Point."

"Absolutely," agreed the doctor.

Ellen heard his chair scoot back from his desk, and then he and her father came through the doorway.

"Ellen!" Dr. George said, smiling. "I swear you're prettier than when I saw you last. You've got a good-looking daughter there, Joe."

"Got Opal's eyes," Joe said proudly.

Ellen only half believed them. If a girl was pretty, people didn't have to go around telling her. She was glad she had washed her hair that morning, though— she liked the feel of it hanging dark and shiny down her back.

"Are you still looking in on the old granny?" Dr. George asked.

"Couple times a week," Ellen told him. "She seems to be doing okay. Swears she takes her medicine."

"Your visits probably do more good than any pills I could give her. Lonely, that's what she is."

Dr. George was a big man, built like a football player, six inches taller than Ellen's father. His hair was snow white, and he had always seemed to Ellen the strongest, smartest man in the backwoods.

"Is Granny Bo's mind still good, Dr. George? I mean, does she ever imagine things?"

"I haven't noticed anything but a little forgetfulness now and then," the doctor said. "Her mind's probably as good as it ever was. Don't underestimate her; she's one smart woman."

"How did her son die?"

Dr. George looked at Ellen thoughtfully. "She told you about him?"

"She said he went off and died."

The doctor thrust his hands in the pockets of his white smock and walked with her to the door.

"She never talks much about that. But if someone tended him on his deathbed, I wasn't the one who was there."

Eight

THE MAN did not come the next morning. Joe Stump had taken the Chevy down to Millville for brake linings, and Ellen washed the shirts he would be needing for his next trip. Jimmy-Clyde came as usual about eleven and went out to Sleet, but there was no sign of Gerald Hawkes around the barn or pasture.

He must have gone, Ellen thought. She watched the crows gathering on top of the barn, raucously trying to edge each other off the end. Then, singly, they went soaring down over the pasture and hid themselves behind the muscadine.

The horse came into view beyond the fence and stood with head fixed, his huge eye on the house. The red hen strutted back and forth on the fence railing, flapping her wings every third step, daring Ellen, it seemed, to come near them. Ellen moved away from the window.

She had kept to her declaration and not gone in the barn again, for it was uncanny the way Sleet seemed to know. Regardless of where he was in the pasture, the moment someone entered his stall—Jimmy-Clyde or Joe—the horse appeared, seemingly out of nowhere. Ellen had only to glimpse the animal through the brush when she went for the mail and instantly she remembered the white of his mad eye as he had galloped, crazed, into the clearing after Billy's fall. She wanted nothing to do with him again, ever.

"You know what?" Jimmy-Clyde said when he came to the house for his three dollars. "You know what? I'm going to a parade on Saturday. A big parade in Millville."

"I've heard about it," said Ellen. "It's the opening of the new auditorium."

"With drums," Jimmy-Clyde said. "A big parade."

"You'll have a lot of fun," Ellen told him.

"Are you going?"

"I don't think so. There's a lot to do here."

The afternoon was half over when Ellen looked out the window and saw Gerald Hawkes making his way across the pasture. She stood on the porch as he came out of the barn with a hammer, but he did not acknowledge her, simply began repairing the loose boards on the shed.

Ellen finally walked out to him and stood some distance away.

"Thought maybe you'd moved on," she said.

He didn't answer for a moment. Then: "Had some problems with Dorothy this morning. Figured I'd better stay around awhile longer."

Ellen waited.

"Aren't you afraid she'll run off or something when you're not there?" she asked finally.

He shook his head. "Pretty scared of things outside the door. Won't even set foot on the porch." The hammering went on, and Ellen drew closer.

"Would it help if I went over and stayed with her a bit? Talked to her, maybe?"

He glanced at her quickly and scowled. "Worst thing in the world you could do. She don't take to strangers at all. I'm just hoping she'll recognize her own sister when I get her to Biloxi." He turned his back on Ellen and began pounding away in earnest.

Ellen saw something of herself in Gerald Hawkes: awkward at social conversation, ill-at-ease among strangers. His abruptness merely made her more determined. At least, she thought dryly, they could practice sociability on each other.

She walked around into his line of vision. "Did you ever try putting her in a hospital?"

Gerald stared at her without straightening up, and Ellen wondered if she had gone too far. He hammered in still another nail, then stared at her again.

"Once," he said finally. "State hospital over in Jordan Springs. But I couldn't stand how they treated her. Tied her to her chair with bedsheets. Couldn't let 'em do that way to Dorothy." He went in the barn for another handful of nails, and this time, when he came out asked:

"Your dad leave on another trip?"

"Leaves Sunday. He's down in Millville right now getting the brakes worked on."

Ellen realized the minute she said it she had told him too much—realized that at that particular moment, in fact, she was alone with him, and Turbo nowhere about. The dog had taken off for the woods that morning, and Ellen hadn't seen him since. But if Gerald had sinister intentions, he kept them to himself and went on working. She began to relax.

"I bet this job of Dad's will take him to almost every city in the state of Mississippi," she said. "Farthest I've ever been in my life is Jackson. It's a great day in the morning when I even get down to Millville."

"Lord, girl, you sure do need to get away."

"It's funny," Ellen told him, "but I feel as though I *have* been away—that I can hear about almost anyplace on TV and come close to believing I've been there."

"It's not the same."

"I know, but . . . well, have you heard about that film producer who's coming to Millville—Robert Cory? He's got this big house in California, right on the ocean —so close you could almost jump off the edge of the yard and dive in. I only saw it on television, but it's like I was really there, standing right at the edge of the cliff in all those clouds."

Gerald Hawkes lifted another board in place and hit the nail hard with his hammer. "Some folks have so much money it almost eats them up, and others don't have enough to spit at," he said.

He worked awhile then without talking, and Ellen poked around for buckberries in the bushes near the shed, slipping the few she found in her pocket.

"You watch TV a lot?" Gerald asked finally.

"TV's broken."

"Read the newspaper?"

"Only paper we get is what's wrapped around the meat from Gacy's store."

Turbo came charging back just then, panting, and covered with burrs.

"Look at you!" Ellen scolded. "You've got yourself a mess of ticks too, I'll bet."

She crouched down beside him and began plucking at the nettles in his coat. She had just finished his left side when she was conscious of something watching her. She glanced up.

The dark horse stood not five feet away on the other side of the fence. The nostrils began salmon-pink at the openings and disappeared into blackness. The ears flicked nervously back and forth, the tail lashed from side to side. Gerald seemed not to notice.

Ellen rose up slowly, edging away, her heart beating rapidly, fear constricting her throat.

"Come, Turbo," she murmured, and started toward the house.

Impulsively, she turned toward the horse once more to glimpse his eye, his awful eye, and saw for the first time that the black stripe running the length of his back from mane to tail was identical to the dark streak that ran through Gerald Hawkes' hair, beginning at the forehead and ending at the nape of the neck.

Ellen felt crippled by her fear of the animal. First it had been the barn where she would not go. Now she avoided the fence as well. Soon she would find it difficult even to step out in the clearing, and already she had transferred that fear to Gerald. She fought against it, but each time the terror returned, it was stronger still.

On Saturday, Joe offered to drive her to the parade in Millville; but Ellen, knowing he wanted to finish some work before leaving the next day, declined. When Beth Larkin called at ten, however, and said that her father was taking her down and could pick up Ellen too, Ellen forced herself to say yes.

"Might as well keep Beth company," she said at the door of the parlor where Joe was going over the contents of his sample case.

"You do that, honey, and have a good time. Buy yourself something while you're in Millville."

She hesitated, struggling with the temptation to call it off, wondering whether—if she stayed home—she might possibly talk her father out of his trip. Immediately, however, she chided herself for her selfishness.

The lane was still muddy, and Ellen walked out to the road to wait for Beth. She could hear the hooves of the dark horse following her along the other side of the muscadine, but she kept her eyes on the mailbox and didn't stop until she had reached Crow's Point Road. When the Larkin's pickup came into view and stopped, engine idling, Ellen went around on the other side and got in.

"We'll probably be the only people watching,"

Beth joked, sliding over to make room. "Everybody else is taking part. Did you know that the mayor's going to give Robert L. Cory the key to the city?" She laughed wickedly. "Can't you just *see* that, Ellen—giving Robert Cory the key to Millville?"

She stretched out her tanned legs beneath her denim skirt, her toes pretty in a pair of sandals. Ellen drew her own feet, in worn sneakers, back under the seat. She realized that she had put on the first thing she had happened to find in her closet, while Beth had dressed with more care. And when Beth reached in her pocket and took out a comb, Ellen realized that all she had in her own pocket were the tweezers she carried to use on Turbo and matches to light the wood stove. It was partly this, she knew—her own feelings of ineptness—that kept her up there on Crow's Point. If Ellen looked in the mirror at all in the mornings, she figured that whatever she saw was the best she could hope for.

"Heard they're going to make his old house over on Magnolia Street a historic monument," Beth said. "Try to make it look like it did back in the days his father owned it."

"Lots of houses around older than his," Ellen commented. "They ought to take a look at our house."

Beth laughed.

Mr. Larkin was a stoop-shouldered man who bent wordlessly over the steering wheel, maneuvering around turns and over hills as he'd done all his life. Cars were already streaming into Millville, and Beth's mother and sisters had gone in early that morning to run a bake sale.

The girls found a place to sit on the wall of the library across from the new auditorium. Ellen studied the building with its white oval dome. A huge banner over the entrance read, "We love you, Robert L. Cory." She remembered the excitement she had felt the time she had gone to see *The Music Man*. It *would* be nice to come down to Millville now and then and see something live on stage, something the folks in New York could go see every night of the year if they wanted. She began to think maybe she loved Robert L. Cory too, and she'd never even met him.

"Figure he'll come in a Cadillac," someone was saying behind her, as more people squeezed up on the wall. And another answered, "Naw, a Rolls Royce. He wouldn't look twice at a Cadillac."

It didn't seem much like Millville. A camera crew moved about on the sidewalk, and cables were stretched from the small platform constructed on the auditorium steps to vans parked nearby.

"Oh, Beth, look! It's *her*!" Ellen gasped suddenly.

Maureen Sinclair was standing in front of a camera, a microphone in one hand. Every so often she gestured toward the parade that was beginning down the street, or at the crowd, or the auditorium, and the camera scanned whatever it was she was talking about. Maureen Sinclair smiled into the lens naturally, talking enthusiastically, and seemed as much at home here in Millville as she had in the television studio back in Merwyn City.

It didn't take long for the parade to pass: the Millville High School Band, the 4-H Club float, the Veterans of Foreign Wars, the Rotary Club, and the fire truck.

And then there were cries of "He's coming! He's coming!"

A black car cruised slowly up to the steps of the auditorium, preceded by Dwight Ruggles, the sheriff, on his motorcycle. The crowd strained to see.

"It's a Lincoln Continental," said a spectator behind Ellen.

A short man got out. He wore no tie, but his clothes were expensive-looking and different from what they wore in Millville. He was not particularly handsome, but he had a warm smile, a lined face that looked as though he had seen everything in the world worth seeing. A pretty young woman got out next, and then a small boy. Together they went up the steps to the platform where the mayor gave them the "key" to the city—tied with a white bow. The crowd clapped. And then Robert L. Cory was at the microphone.

"You know," he said to the crowd, smiling broadly, "I haven't been back to Millville for thirteen years, but there's not a play I've seen or an orchestra I've heard that I haven't thought, someday I want Millville to have this too."

Polite applause.

He went on to talk about roots, how important it was to remember where you came from, and how he'd be forever grateful to the drama department of Millville's Community College where he got his start. Mrs. Cory stood in the background, and the little boy, who had stared wide-eyed at the crowd for a time, began to fidget. He pointed to the television vans and whispered to his mother. People smiled at them, and his mother smiled back. The sun moved behind a cloud, and the landscape turned a shade darker. A breeze played with the silk scarf around Mrs. Cory's neck.

"And now my dream's come true," Robert Cory was saying. "We've got an auditorium in Millville, and every month you're going to get one of the shows they see on Broadway. What you do with the auditorium the rest of the time is up to you, but if I know Millville, there are going to be dancers and singers and poets and actors coming and going in all directions."

The crowd laughed.

"You've got *me* so booked for the next two days, I don't know whether *I'm* coming or going," he said, to more laughter. "But this is something I've wanted to do for a long, long time—to show my son Jason the town I came from, the people I grew up with—something every father ought to do. And so, without more ceremony, it gives me enormous pleasure to dedicate the new auditorium."

The mayor handed him a pair of scissors, and Robert Cory handed them, in turn, to his son. With great concentration, the four-year-old cut the ribbon stretched across the entrance, and the people applauded. The mayor shook hands with the Corys, and the crowd surged toward the steps for the rest of the festivities inside.

At that moment, Ellen saw an arm reach up from the crowd at one side of the platform and tap Jason Cory on the leg. The child bent down and accepted something from an old woman. As his mother moved over and took Jason's hand, Granny Bo turned, making her way through the throngs of people, and disappeared.

Nine

ELLEN STOOD at the door of her father's bedroom while he combed his hair. The uncertain, hollow feeling that had plagued her the day before had been replaced with something more definite. She fought against it, but the feeling was there: anger.

"Better take an umbrella," she cautioned. "Never know what it's planning to do a week from now."

Joe Stump took an old umbrella off the shelf and put it in his suitcase. "Just hope the weather holds till I get down out of these hills. Got an appointment tomorrow to see the motel man in Vicksburg. Once I make that, I can go my own pace up the river."

"Well, you take care, and drive like everybody else is crazy," Ellen reminded him, something her mother used to say.

She was angry that he was going, that he would even think of leaving her there alone. Something wasn't right, but she couldn't put her finger on it. Granny Bo showing up in Millville; Ellen's father going off, one trip on the heels of another; the gossip. . . . It was as though someone knew something that Ellen didn't.

At the same time, Ellen was angry with herself. Hadn't she persuaded her father, when he first brought

it up, that she'd be fine up here alone? Hadn't she reasoned that if Gerald Hawkes meant to harm her, he
would have done so by now? Didn't her father probably
feel that Ellen was safer with Gerald around to watch
over things than if she were here by herself?

"Any man that keeps to his work like that, not
having to be told every second what to do, has got to
have good family in his blood," Joe had commented the
day before. "Dad used to say that Ison Hawkes could
work the legs off a mule, then carry it home on his
shoulders."

"Well, hope I can think up enough work to keep
Gerald busy till you get back," Ellen said. "Don't see
how he can trust his wife over there all alone, though."
She watched her father fold an extra pair of trousers
and lay them on top of his shirts. "What's the state hospital like over in Jordan Springs? Some awful kind of
place?"

"Don't know what it used to be, but they closed it
down five years ago. I worked up there the summer I
laid bricks. Never heard anyone say anything about it,
though. Why?"

"Gerald's wife was there, and he took her out because they mistreated her."

"Some folks have more than their share of hard
luck," Joe said. "If the hospital couldn't help her, sure
don't give him much room for hope, does it?"

Ellen crossed the hall to the kitchen and finished
packing her father's lunch. She had baked a turkey the
day before, and now she cut off slices to wrap in waxed
paper. Gerald was sure going to get his fill of turkey this
week.

"What you going to do with a whole turkey,

Ellen?" Tom Gacy had asked when Ellen ordered it over the phone. "You folks fixing to have some company?"

Ellen had to think quickly. "Dad's going on a selling trip," she answered. "I'm going to send him off with a bunch of sandwiches and make me a stew with the rest."

Tom Gacy had laughed. "I'll send up a small one, then, but you and Joe will be working on that bird till Christmas."

Now Ellen tried to concentrate on the work before her, but resentment had settled in her chest and wouldn't go away. What further angered her was that her father would probably spend more on gas and travel expenses than he would ever earn selling Acme calendars, eternal or otherwise. Even Ellen could see that. Joe Stump never admitted to failure until it fell in his lap, and by that time he'd have his eye on something else. Whatever he chose next, you could be sure, would be the "opportunity of a lifetime." Ellen crammed a turkey sandwich in the bottom of the sack. A person should have so many lifetimes!

On her way back out, she stopped and glanced at her reflection in the mirror over the sink. Green eyes stared back above the angry pink of her cheeks. *Either say something or don't,* she told herself. She should either tell her father how she felt and ask him not to go, or she should reassure him that she would be all right— not just send him off with misgivings. Ellen took a deep breath and went out on the porch where Joe was carrying his suitcase to the car.

"You'll look in on Granny Bo while I'm gone, won't you?" he asked as they crossed the clearing.

"Yes," Ellen promised. "Thought I'd take her some of this turkey before it up and walks away."

"Good idea. Folks livin' alone never cook right for themselves. Gets tiresome."

They reached the old Chevy under the beech tree, and Ellen held the door open while Joe slipped his suitcase inside.

"You ever know any of her children?" she asked.

"Granny Bo's? Went to school with her older boy."

"What was he like?"

Joe shrugged. "Oh, I don't know. A regular sort of fellow."

"Not all spooked and full of superstition like Granny?"

Joe laughed and put his arms around Ellen. "Old folks get like that sometimes, Ellen, just to give their minds somethin' to play on." He hugged her. "What you want me to bring you from Vicksburg? Nothing ordinary, now. Name somethin' fancy."

Ellen tried to think of the fanciest thing she'd ever heard about. "Pheasant under glass," she said.

"What in the world is that?"

She laughed. "I don't know. You always read it's what rich people are having. Pheasant under glass and cherries jubilee."

"Well, we got the pheasants and we got the cherries. Might have to wait a while longer for the glass and jubilee. Listen, girl, I got me a feeling that this time I'm going to hit it big," Joe told her confidently. "Going to send you off to high school this fall looking like all the other girls do—better'n the other girls."

"What you talking about, Dad? We're not poor," Ellen chided.

He laughed. "Honey, we sure ain't rich." The smile faded slightly. "No, indeedy, we sure ain't rich." He got in the car then, and his face seemed determined, his mouth set. "But *this* time it's going to be different. *This* time I got plans."

He reached out and squeezed her arm. "This'll be the last big trip for a long time if everything works out. I promise. See you in a week—sooner, if I can make it."

"Don't worry about me. I'll be fine," Ellen told him.

❦

She sat on the steps with Turbo for a long while after he had gone. It was still very early, and there was fog over the meadow. The jasmine on one side of the porch gave off its perfume, but Ellen scarcely noticed. She found her mind on Granny Bo again. It wasn't just what she heard at Gacy's. It was the whispers and rumors she had grown up with all her life about the old woman—Grannny Bo's spells and potions: witchcraft, some called it.

Cow's horn, poke root, and red alder tea, people clucked.

"Nonsense," Mother had said, laughing at Granny's tonics, which seemed so ominous to others. But Mother wasn't here to laugh now.

Over the years, Granny Bo had become something of a recluse, and the less people saw of her in Millville, the less they talked. Some even assumed she was dead. But each time she made an appearance at Gacy's, a small wrinkled woman in rubber galoshes, straddling an old mule, people passing would ask each other where she could be going; and because they didn't know, they made the answers up.

"Up to no good, I'll bet," they'd say, and whatever misfortune befell anyone at all that week, it was somehow laid to Granny Bo.

When Gerald Hawkes came across the pasture, Ellen could see his legs before she saw the top of him. The fog had risen to waist level, and he looked like the headless horseman. Turbo rose up, then wagged his tail.

Ellen noticed the dark horse following Gerald across the barnyard, its gait keeping time, it seemed, with the man's step. When Gerald got to the fence, he said something to Sleet, and the horse stood motionless, as though waiting for his return. Ellen reached out and put one hand on Turbo.

"Your dad go off?" Gerald asked, coming toward the steps.

She nodded. "May come home early, though. Might just stay a day or two and come back." She wondered if he could tell she was lying.

Gerald studied her. "Think you'll be okay here by yourself?"

Ellen's fingers tightened on Turbo's collar. "Dog would kill anyone who tried to hurt me."

The man looked down at Turbo. "What kind of work have you got?"

"I guess you could chop some firewood."

Watching from the side window while she ate breakfast, Ellen was reassured at the steady way Gerald went about his task. She felt foolish for her uneasiness and relieved that she had not said anything about it to her father. More than that, there was a need to talk to someone, and Ellen reasoned that if she could just draw Gerald out, he might seem less threatening.

On impulse, she dragged the big galvanized wash-tub to the old stump near the woodpile, then filled it with boiling water, returning several times to the kitchen for another kettle full. Gerald stopped working and watched her.

"What you fixing to do?"

"Wash some things."

"Haven't got a washing machine?"

"Yes, but the curtains are fiberglass. You put those in the machine, and they give off little slivers that prick your skin."

Gerald grunted.

"Mother bought them," Ellen said by way of explanation, and then fell silent as she added the soap.

Gerald began hacking away at the wood again, and for a time both of them worked without talking. Ellen stirred the water with a stick, then dropped in the load of curtains.

"What happened to your ma?" Gerald asked at last.

"Spinal meningitis. She was sick for a week, and then died."

He made no answer.

"I lost my brother, too."

Gerald looked over at her. "Same thing?"

"No. He was riding Sleet, and the horse bolted. Billy fell off and hit his head on a rock. A little over a year ago."

Gerald whistled through his teeth. "You've had some *kind* of trouble."

It was about the kindest thing he had said to her so far. "I guess so. But the worst part . . . I mean, the scary part is . . . that someone predicted it. Mother's death."

"Who?"

"An old woman down in the hollow. She told Dad to prepare himself to be a widower, and it wasn't long after that Mother died."

"Could have been a coincidence."

"That's what I keep telling myself. But after Billy died, she said the devil came out of some old crazy man and got in the horse, and that's why he bolted. Does sort of make you wonder."

"Who's the old woman?"

"Granny Bo, we call her. Alma Goff's her real name."

Gerald's ax seemed to pause a second longer, then came crashing down, splitting the wood in three places. "She live alone?"

"Yes. She had three husbands and some children, but they're all dead or moved away. A lot of people say she puts spells on folks and stuff."

"People will believe anything."

"I know, but it still bothers me." Ellen lifted a curtain on the end of the stick and watched the steam rise from it, then let it fall back into the water. "Since Billy died, I haven't been able to go near Sleet. I mean, I have this thing about it. . . . And the longer I stay away, the worse the fear gets. It's so bad now, I can't even go in the barn. I look at Sleet, and I see the devil."

"Best you get rid of him, then."

Ellen shook her head. "Dad would never sell him.

That horse was everything to Billy. Dad just wouldn't feel right letting him go."

Gerald didn't answer. The ax swung again, and the chips flew. The muscles on his arms stood out, and he seemed to crave work the way some men craved drink.

"Which one of the Hawkes' brothers was your father?" Ellen asked after a minute.

Gerald made no answer, and Ellen tried turning it into a compliment: "Dad said he could tell you had good family in your blood, the way you work around here. He said that Ison Hawkes could work the legs off a mule, then carry it home on his shoulders. Was Ison your dad?"

Gerald answered without looking at her: "Yeah." He turned his back on her then, the way he signaled that a conversation was over, and whatever he was thinking, he kept to himself.

Leaving a sack lunch on the kitchen table for Gerald, Ellen went to Granny Bo's around eleven, not because she wanted to but because she had to. Whenever they knew that the old woman had been out riding her mule, the Stumps felt obligated to check up on her, see that she got back all right. Her cabin was far out in the hills, and no one else paid a visit except Dr. George, and that was only on occasion.

How many knew, winding up through the hills from Millville, that a narrow overgrown path beneath a certain thornapple tree went twisting and turning back through the underbrush two miles or so before Alma Goff's cabin came into view? The thornapple itself stood along a dead-end road, so distant from any living soul that it was easier for Ellen, up on Crow's Point, to go down the back way—inland, hill over hill—to Granny's cabin, than for anyone else to try to get in on the weed-choked path below.

There was something about the path up over the bluff, however—the one Ellen took—that even Turbo did not like. He whined when he got to the top and saw that Ellen was going down the other side. Then he tagged along close beside her, ears up, muscles tensed. And when they came to the place where Billy had died, it seemed to Ellen that Turbo moved closer still, brushing against her legs.

Once beyond that point, however, they were out of the darker part of the woods, and the rolling hills stretched before them. Turbo concentrated once again on the scent of fox and jack rabbit and coon. By the time Ellen could see the roof of the old granny's cabin, she decided she was actually looking forward to a cup of tea and bread with blackberry jam.

Does she live alone? Gerald Hawkes had asked, and Ellen wondered why she thought of that now, then wondered whether she should have told him. Well, if he hadn't hurt her, he wasn't likely to hurt an old woman either. Nothing in either house that would interest him in the least.

The mule was hitched to a tree in the side yard. Either Granny Bo had hitched him up when she got back the day before and not put him out to pasture yet, or she was getting ready to go somewhere again.

"Granny Bo?" Ellen called, knocking on the screen. There was no sound from inside, however. Alarmed,

Ellen began to pound. A bent figure made its way toward her.

"Like to wake the devil!" the woman half-scolded.

"I'm sorry. When you didn't come, I got worried. Usually you're waiting for me on the porch."

"I catch me a nap now and then, is all." Granny Bo said. "Sit you down." She accepted the package of turkey meat Ellen had brought and went back to the kitchen. It was some time before she appeared again, but when she did she had a slice of bread cut in four sections, smeared with jam, and a mason jar full of cold tea, which she poured into glasses.

"What is this?" Ellen asked, sipping the tea warily.

"Squaw mint," said Granny. "Good for whatever ails you."

Ellen looked out over the yard where suckers sprayed up from the stump of a black locust tree. "Have you been out riding Georgia?" she asked, nodding toward the mule.

"Yep. Rode her to Millville yesterday and down along the creek today. Best to keep in practice so the muscles don't tighten up."

Ellen helped herself to the bread. "How did you like the parade?"

"Lot of noise about nothing."

"You don't like the Cory Auditorium?"

"Good for us and bad for him," Granny Bo said.

Ellen studied her. "Why?"

"Guilt brings him back, that's why." She beat her gums together a time or two before continuing: "Robert Cory made his money in cattle—his daddy did, anyway.

Cattle and pecans. And then he ups and moves to California. Didn't profit the folks of Millville, him moving. Now he's back, rich and famous, and builds us an auditorium. You think all those fancy actors from New York are going to bother with us? In six months won't be nothin' playin' but shows put on by the Millville fire department."

Ellen laughed. "Well, it's better than no auditorium at all." A cackle of crows came from somewhere off in the woods.

"Not good to come back to your own people carryin' a load of guilt," Granny Bo predicted. "Trying to make up for movin' out on us, and he don't fool a soul. Soon as the speechifyin's over, he'll hightail it back to California, and we'll not see him again."

Ellen shrugged. "Even if he doesn't come back, it seems like a pretty nice thing to do for Millville."

"Maybe," said Granny Bo, and then, tightlipped, rocked back and forth in her chair, lifting her feet slightly each time the chair went back and putting them down again with a thud.

"What did you give to his little boy?" Ellen asked.

Granny Bo stopped rocking and looked at her hard. "What's that?"

"I was just curious." Ellen tried to sound casual. "I saw you reach up and hand something to Robert Cory's son."

"A penny, that's all," Granny said, rocking again. "Give him something to amuse him while all the speeches were goin' on inside." She folded her hands, obviously done with the conversation, and concentrated on Ellen again. "How's your father?"

"All right. He's on another one of his business trips. Will be gone a whole week."

Granny Bo's eyes seemed to darken. "Not a good time," she said, as if to herself. "Not a good time at all." A raindrop pinged on the roof of the porch, then another. And then there was silence.

"I'm getting along just fine," Ellen said quickly. "We've got a new neighbor. . . ." She stopped, remembering Gerald's request. She could not back down now, but at least she would keep his sick wife a secret. "He's staying at the old Brody place for a few days and comes over to help out. Sort of looks after things while Dad's gone."

"He from Millville?"

"No, one of Ison Hawkes's boys, up near the Tennessee line."

Granny Bo cocked her head suddenly, the rocker gone still, and her fingers twitched in her lap—a jerky, agitated motion.

"No," she said deliberately. "Not one of Ison's boys. Ison had him six daughters and two sons, and three—four—years ago, both of 'em drowned."

Her withered, knobby fingers drummed against her knee, and then she began rocking again, her eyes on Ellen.

And Ellen, sitting motionless in her chair, felt caught between the cabin there in the hollow and the bluff back up on the trail. She knew she could not stay in the cabin, and she was afraid to go home.

Ten

SHE STUMBLED back up the path, her throat dry, her hands cold. Each snap of twig, every rustle of leaf brought her to an abrupt stop, and she waited, heart pounding, till Turbo moved on.

Ellen did not know where the danger lay, but danger there was, she was sure of it. Granny Bo was holding something back—Ellen could sense it, and Gerald had not told her the truth. When she reached the steep rocky path at the end of the journey, the house waiting there on the other side seemed more like a trap than a refuge. Where else could she go?

She could call Beth Larkin and ask if she could stay overnight with her—stay all week, in fact. Take Turbo, too. She could call the sheriff. Yet what would she tell him, or anyone else? That she was frightened? Of what? they would ask. She didn't know.

At the crest of the bluff, the sky opened wide around her. Thickening clouds were churning up billows of gray. Ellen thought of her father. Surely he had made it down to the delta by now and would go safely on to Vicksburg.

The wind grew stronger as she crossed the ridge and started down the other side. Why hadn't her father remembered that Ison Hawkes's sons were drowned?

Even now Ellen could conjure up a dim memory of talk about it at Gacys'—about *somebody* drowning, anyway, up near Pickwick Dam. And then she realized that it wasn't Joe who had asked Gerald which of the Hawkeses was his father. It was Ellen herself who had asked. Her father probably assumed that Gerald belonged to one of the other brothers, not Ison.

She felt terrified suddenly of being alone with Gerald and made it to the porch just as she saw him coming through the gate at the end of the pasture.

A low rumble of thunder came from the east.

Gerald glanced up at the sky and went immediately to work on the short stretch of fence between barn and shed, pulling up the rotted posts and digging holes for new ones. A little later Ellen heard his footsteps on the porch.

"Ellen?"

Her heart raced. "Yes?"

He didn't answer, waiting instead for her to come out. She moved toward the door of the parlor. Outside, the sky was darker still.

"I did all I could on those fence posts, but they won't last a week 'less we get some cement down in there. Your dad's got a bag out here in the shed. You reckon he'd mind if I used it?"

"I don't suppose so." Ellen waited for the pounding of her heart to subside.

"I'll pour it tomorrow then. No use startin' now with a storm on the way."

The thunder grew louder, and a streak of lightning zigzagged across the sky.

"Nothing much you can do here in the rain," Ellen agreed quickly. "Why don't I give you supper early, and you go on back? It'll be a cold meal this time— we're still working on that turkey. Wait here and I'll get it."

She went to the kitchen, throwing things together haphazardly.

He was still standing on the porch as she'd left him, his back to the sky, his face in shadow, and it was impossible to know what he was thinking.

He took the sack but still made no move to leave. "Anything wrong?" It was a polite inquiry, but his voice was as cold as steel.

Ellen shook her head. "Storms always make me nervous—after what happened to Billy." Her own voice sounded high, tight. "You go on—get back before the rain hits."

But it was too late. Lightning lit up the entire sky as an explosive clap of thunder almost deafened her. For a moment the huge beech tree on the lawn seemed aflame, and then slowly, the left half of the trunk began ripping, cracking, and started to fall. Ellen screamed. With a huge boom it hit the ground, the white bark ripped in one seam along the trunk from top to bottom. Turbo yelped.

And then, before Ellen could catch her breath, there was a loud whinny from the dark horse, and he crashed through the new fence posts, which had sat propped but unsecured in their open holes. A moment later the huge animal galloped into the clearing toward the house, mane flying, eyes wild, hooves scraping and digging into the bare earth. Ellen shrieked in terror.

On he came, clattering against the steps, dancing out into the clearing, then lunging, hooves banging, toward Ellen once more. Turbo ran around in circles on the porch, barking hysterically. Ellen fell on him and held him to her.

When the horse came again, the white froth spewing out one side of its mouth, Gerald Hawkes leaped off the steps. The horse reared up, huge, showing the white of its eyes, ears laid back, nostrils flared, sides heaving.

Ellen was too terrified to watch. She crouched near the door, head turned away, arms around Turbo, the only one she could trust. She could feel the vibration of Sleet's hooves against the earth, hear Gerald's exclamations. The rain came, lashing sideways, drumming hard against the tin roof of the porch.

There were more whinnies from beyond the steps, the sound of a struggle, and then a sharp command. And finally there was quiet, except for the roar of the storm and the horse's panting. When Ellen raised her head again, Sleet was standing still, his dark coat sleek and wet. Gerald patted his side, one hand secure on his mane. He turned, leading the horse into the barn, and Ellen heard the clank of the bolt, shutting the door fast. The wind rose and fell, and the rain pelted down, slacked, then came again. Once more lightning flashed and thunder cracked. Sleet whinnied from the barn.

Gerald came back to the porch and picked up his sack, his clothing drenched.

"Spooked, that's all," he said, still breathless.

Ellen could not trust herself to reply. She could hear his loud breathing, smell the damp of his leather boots.

"Looks like you only got about half a tree left," Gerald went on. "Your dad's going to be mighty sorry to lose that beech."

Ellen found herself shaking even more violently than before.

"You okay?" Gerald said at last.

"Yes, really. Please go," Ellen said.

And when she raised her head again, the man was gone. She could see nothing but rain beyond the barn, as though the storm had swallowed him up.

❧

The storm passed as quickly as it had begun, yet long after the rain ended, Ellen sat at the window like a guard on lookout, watching for the slightest sign that she should take Turbo and flee. She stared at the meadow and the gate beyond until evening fell and it was finally too dark to see at all.

If only her father were there. If only he would call. Every so often the phone gave a slight, almost imperceptible beep, as it did when anyone else on the party line was dialing a call. Twice it actually rang, but it was someone else's ring. Even this, however, was a comfort to Ellen, to know that if she lifted the receiver, she would hear a human voice, someone she knew. Once or twice she longed to lift the receiver and join in the conversation just to connect herself to somebody.

She imagined her father there in the room with her and what he would say if she told him she didn't know what to be afraid of most: Gerald or Sleet or Granny Bo's pronouncements or even the old woman herself. She remembered that thin, withered arm reaching up to tap Jason Cory on the leg, the way Mrs. Cory had taken Jason's hand, shrinking back—the anxious way she had smiled at Granny Bo.

"She *does* see things," Ellen would tell her father if he were there. "She sees trouble before it even happens. Something is about to happen now and I don't know what."

You wait long enough, something always happens, her father would say. *She's probably upset about that new auditorium. Old folks don't like things to change, like everything to stay just the way they remember it.*

Ellen hugged her knees and shivered, chilled by the damp night air.

"But what about Gerald? If he's not one of Ison Hawkes's boys, why did he tell me he was?" That's what she would ask her father next.

Even if he is someone else, don't mean he's out to do you no harm, Joe would answer.

Ellen wasn't entirely sure that's what her father would say, but it was close. Being here alone, without anyone to sort things out with, did things to her mind.

By the time she turned on the light, she was beginning to feel better. She went methodically around latching the doors in the kitchen and parlor, checking the windows, and then, normal precautions having been taken, set about making supper for herself.

She missed the television, for one thing—missed the sound of familiar voices. Once there had been an old radio around the place, but she didn't know where it was. She tried singing, something her mother used to do, but Ellen's voice was out of tune and Turbo looked at her uncertainly. She laughed aloud and was cheered by the sound of it.

The uneasiness returned when it was time to go

across the hall to bed, but she made a dash for it, then locked herself in with Turbo.

For a long time, however, sleep did not come. Ellen propped herself up on pillows so that she could look out over the edge of the windowsill. There was only darkness beyond, yet she felt that if something *did* pass by, she might see it.

As the night wore on and she turned restlessly, new worries took over. What if Gerald Hawkes *was* one of Ison's boys, and they *had* been drowned, and the "haints" Granny Bo talked about had taken up residence here?

She moaned in the terror she had created and forced herself to sit up.

"Stop it," she said to the imaginings that pounded in her head. "Ellen April Stump, you are so ridiculous."

It was then she heard it—a night cry. It was like nothing she had ever heard before, for it seemed cut off in the middle—a human sound not made by any human she knew. And in the quiet that followed, Ellen seemed to see her father's face there on the opposite wall.

Eleven

THE NEXT MORNING, when it became nine, then ten, and Gerald still had not appeared, Ellen hoped that he had gone on, whoever he was, and taken his wife with him. But the next time she looked out, he was chopping up the fallen limbs of the beech tree. He worked rhythmically, swinging the ax, then bending over to put the smaller branches in a pile.

She went out to him at last. Several branches from the pecan tree had fallen too, and the pecans, in their greenish leathery shells, were scattered about the yard like miniature footballs.

"Any more trouble with the horse?" he asked her.

"No. Once the thunder passes, he's quiet."

Gerald went on working.

Ellen walked around, picking up stray branches, piling them on top of the brush heap. She chose her words carefully:

"I'm thinking maybe Dad'll drive back in tonight. He said if he got a big enough order in Vicksburg, he might just come on home." Then, without looking at him, Ellen asked casually. "You ever see your father? Ison?"

She could feel Gerald's eyes studying her.

"No."

"I was just thinking about your wife, I guess," Ellen chattered on, "wondering why your own kin don't help you take care of her."

Gerald went on chopping. "Maybe we don't get along," he said, and volunteered nothing more. Ellen did not dare carry it further.

Again, however, the steadiness of his work impressed her, as it had her father. Maybe he was a man besieged with bad luck and was trying to make a new life for himself. Maybe he had taken on someone else's name so his creditors couldn't follow him to Biloxi.

There could be a dozen reasons, none of them any of her business. And maybe Granny Bo's memory had failed her and it was somebody else's sons who had drowned.

The phone had been ringing all morning, it seemed, but not for her. Each time it jangled, she thought it might be her father. If only he'd call. She wondered where he was right then, whether he had made his appointment on time with the motel man, whether the storm that had struck last night had yet reached Vicksburg.

What she tried not to think about was the night cry, but no matter how occupied she kept her mind, the thought seeped back in again like water under a door. *The first person you think of after you hear it, that's the person you ought to fix on,* Granny Bo had said. *Whatever's going to happen, that person figures in it somehow.* Ellen thought of the brakes on her father's car, of the possibility of his going to sleep at the wheel. . . .

The ringing of the phone went on. If it wasn't the loud ring of someone calling in, it was the little cheep as someone dialed out. Strange for a Monday, all this calling, Ellen was thinking.

At one, Gerald came up to the porch and called her.

"Think I'll take my lunch now. Gettin' right hungry. When I come back, I'll pour the concrete in those post holes." He sat down on the porch to wait.

"You want two sandwiches or three?" Ellen asked.

"Make it three."

She packed a large lunch, and Gerald set off.

After he had gone, she turned on the TV just for

the picture before realizing that it was after one and the news was over. She had just started to turn the set off again when Maureen Sinclair appeared on the screen. Ellen looked at the clock on the wall. One-twenty. How strange.

Almost immediately the picture changed to Robert L. Cory. Ellen sensed that something was wrong. He looked very, very old—his hair and clothes disheveled. The camera followed him as he walked in the sheriff's office in Millville, and then Maureen Sinclair was talking again, her face grim.

What on earth could have happened? Ellen tried desperately to read the woman's lips. Had the film producer been arrested? Had the auditorium burned down? She stared at the picture, trying to guess. Now Maureen Sinclair was interviewing Dwight Ruggles. . . .

The phone rang, one long ring and one short. Ellen rushed to answer.

"Ellen!" came Beth's voice. "Have you *heard*?"

"What's happened?" Ellen cried. "Our TV's broken."

"It's Robert Cory's little boy. He's gone!"

"Beth!"

"They think it's a kidnapping. He disappeared last night. I've been trying to call you all morning, but the line was busy."

"I can't believe it!" Ellen said. "How could it have happened?"

"The Corys were staying with old friends in Millville, but they went to a dinner at the mayor's home last night and left Jason behind with the maid. No one heard a thing, but when the Corys and their friends got back, Jason was gone."

"Maybe he just wandered off."

"They don't think so. The window was forced open from the outside."

"But how would anyone know that the Corys weren't there?"

"Oh, Ellen, their whole schedule has been in the newspapers—all the parties, the dinners. Someone's been keeping track."

Ellen leaned against the wall, stunned. "Was there a ransom note?"

"No. At least Dwight Ruggles said there wasn't."

"Dwight Ruggles couldn't find a ransom note if it was pinned to his shirt!" Ellen said indignantly, furious that they had a sheriff who was so inept.

"Now don't you talk that way about Dwight," said a third voice that wasn't Beth's. "I just picked up the receiver to make a call and couldn't help but overhear you girls."

Ellen recognized the voice of Mrs. Conklin.

"Dwight Ruggles is doing the best he can, and we ought to give him all the help he needs."

"Listen," Ellen pleaded to both of them. "Call me if there's any more news at all."

"I will," Beth promised.

"I'll dial you up," Mrs. Conklin offered. "Anything I hear, I'll let you know."

When Ellen saw Gerald working in the yard later, she hurried out to him.

"Something awful's happened!" she said, Turbo running alongside her.

He straightened up. "What's that?"

"Robert Cory. The film producer. His little boy's been kidnapped."

"Kidnapped?" He looked at her intently.

"That's what they think. Jason disappeared last night. A friend just called me."

Gerald shook his head. "Bet Cory never expected a thing like that to happen in Millville."

"Oh, I've got such a horrible feeling," Ellen said.

"Why?"

"You know that old woman I told you about? Granny Bo? She was there at the ceremony. I saw her push through the crowd and give Jason a penny."

Gerald emptied the bag of cement mix on a sheet of metal siding and poured a little water from a pail on top of it, stirring with a stick. "What's so awful about that?"

"Well . . . it just seemed so odd at the time, the way she reached up to him. . . . They say she used to wander the streets of Millville, talking to little boys, giving out pennies. . . ."

"Don't go making more of it than it was," Gerald said, and went for the shovel.

When the phone rang an hour later, Ellen answered immediately.

"Ellen, this is Mrs. Conklin," came the voice. "You said you wanted to know if there was more news."

Ellen was glad to hear even from her.

"What is it?"

"Well, it just occurred to us that maybe you could help. It's about Granny Bo. . . ."

Ellen felt as though her tongue were frozen to the roof of her mouth.

"We all saw Granny Bo in Millville the day of the ceremony, and you have to admit that's unusual."

Ellen found her voice at last. "Lots of folks were there last Saturday that don't get to town much."

"Yes, but we all know she has a fondness for little children, and when a person gets as old as she is, her mind's like to go."

"So what do you think she's done—eaten him?"

Mrs. Conklin gave a weak laugh. "Of course not. But it's entirely possible that in her loneliness she just took him."

"Then for heaven's sake why doesn't Dwight Ruggles drive up there and ask?" Ellen said. The more Mrs. Conklin voiced her fears, the harder Ellen fought against her own. "All this talk behind her back, making her seem like a witch or something."

"Dwight *has* gone up there," said Mrs. Conklin. "As soon as little Jason was discovered missing, everyone said 'Granny Bo,' and Dwight drove right up to Alma's cabin with a county police officer and they searched it through. Didn't find a thing."

"Well, then!" Ellen said, relieved.

"But you know her better than anyone, the way you and your father look in on her," the woman continued. "And we just thought . . . Irene Gacy suggested it, actually . . . that maybe if you went to see Granny Bo, she might tell you something she wouldn't tell Dwight."

"I'll talk to her the next time I go down," Ellen said, "but if the police didn't find any trace of the boy, then I'm sure he's not there. Thanks for calling, Mrs. Conklin."

Ellen hung up and before she could even lift her hand from the receiver, heard the furtive cheep of the phone that meant someone on the line was dialing out. She could not resist listening in:

"Irene?" Mrs. Conklin was saying, "I talked to her, but all I got was sass. Defends the old woman. Made it sound like we were on a witch hunt or something."

"A strange one, that girl—her and her father," Irene shot back. "Alma Goff not talking, Ellen not giving us a bit of help, and Joe Stump not even around. Got his brakes lined last Saturday, they say—went off on a trip somewhere, but did anybody see him leave? It's a funny business, if you ask me."

Ellen softly replaced the receiver. She would have to confront the old woman, and she would have to go alone.

Twelve

ELLEN did not go to Granny Bo's the next day, however. It was not her fear of the old woman or her dread of the wooded path or even what she might discover when she got there. It was something that frightened her more—something that had worked its way up through the layers of consciousness overnight and surfaced clearly, terrifyingly, the next morning.

Her father.

The mere thought of him, the idea, the suspicion, made her double over as if in pain.

Time and again she went over all the remarks he had made about his coming trip, taking them apart word by word, trying to remember his inflection, his face, his intent:

Next week I'll make enough to buy us a color TV, Ellen April . . . Laid the groundwork, you might say . . . I got me a feeling that this time I'm going to hit it big . . . Going to send you off to high school looking like all the other girls do . . . better'n the other girls. . . .

But was that any different from what he always said? He *always* talked big; always promised more than he could deliver. And yet . . . ?

Joe Stump knew Millville like his own front yard—every house, every street, every alley. He knew the surrounding hill country, the winding roads, the turnoffs, the cliffs. . . . How desperately did a man have to want to change his luck before he would resort to a crime like this? Even as she considered it, guilt stabbed at her for her disloyalty. When had her father done anything to make her doubt him? What silly imaginings were these that would make her distrust him, of all people?

"What are you talking about, Dad? We're not poor," Ellen chided. And she remembered the way his smile had faded, the determined look that filled his eye, the set of his jaw: *Honey, we sure ain't rich. . . . But this time it's going to be different. This time I got plans. It'll be the last big trip for a long time if everything works out, I promise.*

Ellen squeezed her arms tightly, forehead on her knees.

Jimmy-Clyde arrived late that morning, just after Gerald had taken lunch back to Dorothy.

"Big excitement!" Jimmy-Clyde said breathlessly, putting the grocery sack on the table. "Boy! Isn't it something? Isn't it something?"

"It's awful," said Ellen.

"Everyone's talking about it," Jimmy-Clyde went on, flicking his tongue out between his lips and pressing the palms of his hands together. "Irene says she knows where Mr. Cory's little boy is."

"That's wonderful," said Ellen. "Why doesn't she go get him, then?"

"Granny Bo's got him," Jimmy-Clyde said seriously. His eyes widened as he spoke, and he flicked his tongue out again. "Granny Bo's got him hid down by the creek."

"Jimmy-Clyde, you shouldn't go around saying things unless you're sure they're true," Ellen reprimanded. "Just because Irene Gacy lets her mouth run on, doesn't mean you have to."

His shoulders hunched defensively the way he did when someone spoke sharply to him, and Jimmy-Clyde marched on out to the barn. Ellen set about putting the groceries away.

At she picked up the ground beef, she unwrapped the layer of newspaper around it. There was Monday's date at the top, and Ellen had to stop and figure out what day it was now. Tuesday. The newspaper was only a day old.

She put the hamburger in the refrigerator and eagerly spread the paper out on the table. Jimmy-Clyde had brought the news section, and there was a story about the disappearance of Jason on the front page:

"Cory Child Missing: Sheriff Suspects Foul Play," was the headline.

Ellen sat down in a chair and read it—how the Corys and their friends had come home on Sunday evening to find Jason gone and a window forced open in his room of the air-conditioned house.

The maid was distraught, the story said, insisting that she had heard no unusual noise or any sound from Jason, though she did seem to remember the noise of a car driving away about ten o'clock and assumed it was a neighbor. The sheriff was checking for fingerprints. Robert Cory was at a loss to explain who might have kidnapped his child, but police planned to question several former business associates who . . .

The rest of the story was continued on A-16. Ellen quickly turned the pages and was dismayed to find that she had only the first twelve pages of the paper. She read the first part again, feeling more reassured that her father was not involved. The article said nothing about suspects around Millville, and who knew what kind of life Robert Cory led in California? There were probably all sorts of people who envied his fame and money.

She felt better then and, after Jimmy-Clyde had cleaned out Sleet's stall and left, she took Turbo and went to the plum trees at the far end of the orchard to gather a basketful for jam. On the other side of the fence, separating the fruit trees from pasture, the dark horse followed her at a distance.

❧❀❧

She picked all she could find on the ground and then climbed up on a lower branch and picked the ones she could reach. She had gathered three-quarters of a basket when she heard Gerald coming along the path through the cedars. She jumped down as he reached the gate.

He spun around, one hand flying up as if to shield himself, and then he saw Ellen.

"Trying to scare me to death?" He glowered.

"I'm sorry. Was picking plums for jam, that's all." She went back toward the house with him, staying on the tree side of the fence while Gerald walked through the pasture.

"Any more news about that kid?" Gerald asked.

"Folks around here think it's Granny Bo. First thing the sheriff did was ride up and search her cabin."

Gerald smiled faintly. "They find anything?"

"Probably a jar of red alder tea and some juniper berries," Ellen told him, dryly.

"No ransom note?"

"Nothing. The boy's just gone."

"That's a strange one, all right."

Ellen desperately needed to talk, to trust—even this stranger with the deep-set eyes.

"Gerald," she said impulsively, "if you were to kidnap a little boy, where would you hide him?"

For a moment he didn't answer. His boots made a crunching, solid sound as he strode heavily through the tall grass, and finally he said, "Well, if it ever occurred to me to do that, I suppose I'd go some place there were a lot of people."

The hollow feeling returned, and Ellen felt it ballooning in her chest. Her eyes fixed on a lizard crawling along the top rail of the fence in the sun.

"Like . . . like Jackson or Vicksburg?" she asked.

"That's it. Some place where they're used to seeing strangers. Around here, people notice you right off."

Ellen left him when she reached the clearing and went on in the house. As she rinsed off the plums, she noticed that her hands were shaking.

It was three when the phone rang—Ellen's ring. She knew, when she lifted the receiver, that other receivers were being lifted as well. Might as well hook the phone up to a loud speaker.

"Ellen," said Beth, "they found a ransom note."

Ellen felt the blood drain from her face. "What did it say?"

"It was taped to the door of Robert Cory's old home on Magnolia Street. Dwight Ruggles found it, and the idiot called the TV station and told them what it said. Said the kidnappers were asking one hundred thousand dollars, and if Cory didn't tell the county police to lay off, he might never see his boy alive again. It said he had three days to deliver the money, and he'd be contacted later about where to leave it."

"Did he . . . did he describe the note?"

"Everything about it. Said it was a piece of paper torn from a yellow, lined tablet and written in blue ink, with a ballpoint pen."

"And the writing . . . ?" Ellen asked, her voice barely audible.

"It was printed—big block-type letters, so as not to give anything away. The county police are furious, and so is Robert Cory. They say Ruggles should never have made the note public."

"Well, I don't know why not." This time the voice

was Grace Talbot's, and she didn't even apologize for listening in. "There's a lot us hill folk know that the police don't; and I say, if anybody solves this, it's going to be us. First thing I did when I heard about the yellow writing paper was call Irene Gacy, and she's making a list of all the people who bought that kind of tablet lately. First name at the top of the list is Granny Bo's."

From where Ellen sat, she could see the small desk her father used over by the window with the tablet of yellow writing paper and the blue ballpoint pen.

There was still another voice on the line, and it was Mrs. Conklin's. The two women took over the conversation.

"Grace, Irene thinks we got to go after Alma Goff ourselves. Says the old woman's as fond of her mule as a mother loves a child; and she thinks we ought to threaten to shoot it, if she don't tell us where she's got the boy hid."

Ellen listened, horrified. "And what if she really doesn't have Jason?" she asked.

"Well, it's only a mule. Not like we was threatening *her*, after all."

"Listen, Beth, call me if you hear anything new," Ellen said.

"I will."

Ellen stood up and huddled, shivering, in the corner by the refrigerator. She could not bring herself to go near the desk and writing tablet.

Suspicions mounted in her mind until there seemed a pyramid of doubt pushing through the top of her head. When her father had stayed home the day of the auditorium's dedication, had he, really? When he drove off Sunday morning, hoping to make Vicksburg, he'd said, by Monday, had he gone at all? Or had he hidden himself away until Sunday evening, then taken the child with him, and probably not to Vicksburg but to Jackson? One thing she was sure of, if he *had* taken the child—out of whatever desperation she couldn't even imagine—he would not harm him. The threat was only a bluff. But why . . . ? Ellen sat down in a chair by the table finally, trembling.

How could he have done it? There was no reason she could think of that matched her father. How could he dream he could bring it off? A hundred-thousand dollars would buy a whole lot of color TV's. He certainly wouldn't do it for that. What would the people of Millville say if the Stumps suddenly bought new furniture and a new car or moved to a condominium in Oxford? No, it made no sense whatsoever. The more she thought about it, the more positive she was that it was entirely out of the question.

She did not know how long she had been sitting there, but a shadow crossed the doorway. She turned.

"Am I gettin' any dinner tonight?" Gerald asked.

"Oh, I forgot!" Ellen stood up quickly. "You want a glass of iced tea while I fix it?"

Turbo trotted over beside Gerald and sat at his feet at the table. The man took a long drink from the glass, then leaned back in his chair.

"Sure is hot. Hotter in Biloxi too, I'll bet."

"Any idea when you'll go?" Ellen asked. The old wood stove was cold, and it was too late to start the hamburger she had planned for supper. Ellen opened a can of tuna instead and mixed it with mayonnaise and celery.

"No," Gerald said. "Dottie's not gettin' a bit better, and I don't see that keepin' her shut up way back here is doin' her any good. Might just have to take a chance, put her in the car, and set off anyway, no matter how she carries on."

"When was she in the hospital at Jordan Springs?" Ellen asked, trying hard to keep the conversation going. She spooned the tuna salad into a plastic container and pushed down hard on the lid.

"Couple years ago," Gerald said.

The container of tuna dropped from Ellen's hands onto the floor. It was as if she could see her father standing there in the room, hear him say, of Jordan Springs, *Don't know what it used to be, but they closed it down five years ago.*

"What's the matter?" Gerald asked, watching her.

She picked up the container again and placed it in the sack. "Clumsy, that's all." The blood throbbed in her temples. "All this kidnapping stuff has my nerves on edge."

He gave a wry smile. "Well, nobody's going to kidnap you, that's for sure. Wouldn't get much for ransom, would they?"

"Sure wouldn't," she said, casting a quick look at Turbo. "A horse, two hens, and Dad's old Chevy—that's about it."

"Any more news?"

She debated how much she should tell him. All her earlier reservations about the man came rushing back. He was lying about his wife being in the state hospital. And if Granny Bo's memory was right, he was lying about being Ison Hawkes's son. Who was he, then? Someone who once knew this hill country well, that's who, and had set his sights on the old Brody house as a place to stay. But he hadn't known about the hospital closing at Jordan Springs, and he hadn't heard about the drowning of Ison's boys. Whoever the man was, he had been away for some time.

"I sure would be the last one to hear if there was anything happening," she told him in answer, and put some cheese and apples in the sack with the rest.

"Nobody called?" Gerald quizzed her, looking at her hard.

"Oh, Beth did. Calls all the time. But it's just gossip. All about Granny Bo."

"Must be some sheriff you've got up here if he can't do better than pick on the old woman," Gerald said, taking the sack.

Ellen cried after he left. Cried out of terror and exhaustion and disappointment and loneliness. A few days before she had felt there was no place she could go where she would be safe. Now she felt there was no person left that she could trust.

How could she protect her father? Throw out the writing pad? She went to the desk and started to pick up the pen, but stopped. She stared down at the tablet, then went to her bedroom and brought back the flashlight. Holding it over the paper in such a way that indentations produced shadow, she could just make out lines that had been written on the page above. She could not read the words, but could tell that they were all printed in block-type letters. She leaned against the wall, eyes closed.

Thirteen

ELLEN lay on the couch in the parlor the next day, ill from worry. Her head ached and she felt sick to her stomach, but the sickness, she knew, was in her heart.

She put leftovers together for lunch and merely set the sack on the steps when she saw Gerald coming.

"I've got flu or something," she lied from the doorway of the parlor.

He nodded, took the sack, disappeared for an hour or so, and then was back working in the yard again.

The incessant ringing of the telephone went on, and now and then there was a call for her, but never the one she wanted; never her father. Mostly the news was no news at all. Dwight Ruggles, stung by criticism from the county police, had no comment about anything. Mrs. Conklin called to say she'd heard that Robert Cory had told both the police and sheriff to let him deal with the kidnappers alone.

"Have you been to see Granny Bo?" she asked.

"No," Ellen told her. "Dad's away, and I've got a lot to do around here. Maybe I can get down there tomorrow."

"Where on earth *is* your father, Ellen?"

"He'll be home soon," Ellen said in answer, and

sat with her forehead on her arms long after she had hung up.

If she could only talk with him, hear her father's voice, she would know whether he was a part of it all. She'd talk him out of it—explain to the police. She would return Jason to his parents, and everything would be all right. And then she wondered if it was possible that Gerald and her father were involved in this together, and she went back to the couch and lay with her face in the pillow.

～～❦～～

A vigilante group, however, was being organized to go see Granny Bo. Ellen heard about it from Beth.

"You should hear them talking, Ellen," she told her over the phone. "Irene Gacy's behind it, of course. Tomorrow afternoon, when the men get home from the mill, they're all going to Granny Bo's—nine of them— and threaten to shoot her mule."

"And if Granny Bo gets wind of it, we'll know who told her," put in Grace Talbot, listening in. "Robert Cory even turned down help from the FBI, says he'll pay the ransom, anything, to get his son back. Well, if the FBI can't help, maybe us folks can."

Ellen went out to sit in the breezeway, not daring to go any further, should her father call. Grace Talbot had a short memory, she was thinking. Just last year someone thought an escaped convict was hiding in Ezra Jeeter's barn. Word got out, and before Dwight Ruggles got halfway up to Crow's Point Road, the Talbot boys had run over and set fire to Ezra's barn, and what they smoked out was a neighbor's goat, singed but otherwise unhurt. Let a vigilante group loose up here, and they'd not only have the mule shot but Granny Bo bound and gagged for want of a better suspect.

She turned on the TV and saw Mrs. Cory, tears in her eyes, face drawn. Ellen turned off the silent set and stared at the phone in the kitchen beyond, as though she could will it to ring. Her head pounded.

At four o'clock she called in an order to Gacy's to be delivered the next day and added a bottle of aspirin to the list.

"Can you hold out till tomorrow, dear, or should I have Jimmy-Clyde run it up this evening?" Mrs. Gacy asked.

"I can wait,"Ellen told her.

There was scarcely enough food in the refrigerator to make a decent supper, but Ellen was too upset to cook. She put the last of the turkey in a sack, set it outside, and wasn't even watching when Gerald came to get it. She fell asleep on the couch in the parlor and slept right through the dinner hour and on into the night.

It was almost five in the morning when she woke. The sleep seemed to have helped, for the headache was gone and her stomach was steady. She lay quietly, enjoying this moment before the worries set in. And then she heard it and sat straight up, as if yanked forward by an invisible hand: the night cry.

She listened, her body taut, straining to hear. The cry came again, and—just as it had five days before—was cut off in the middle. Ellen knew suddenly that whatever else the night cry might be, this cry was that of a frightened child—as clear, as distinct, as if she could see him standing in the meadow. Turbo heard it too, for he rose up on his haunches, ears pricked forward. Goosebumps rose on Ellen's arms, and she could feel her own heartbeat. Jason was out there somewhere.

❧§§❧

Along with the knowledge that the child was near came the certainty that her father had nothing to do with the kidnapping. It was Gerald.

The suspicions she had only toyed with before rose up and filled the room. Until now she had not dared confront them openly, for to do so was to realize that she was trapped up here alone with the man and completely at his mercy. What if she had reported him before to Dwight Ruggles, only to have the sheriff search the old Brody place and find nothing amiss? What would Gerald have done to her then? And in her fears about her father, she had needed so desperately a person she could trust that she had trusted a man she hardly knew. No more. But she had to make sure.

Ellen felt around for her shoes. She had always liked early morning. It seemed to her that she felt more acutely, thought more distinctly in the hours just around sunrise. By the time she drank some juice, she had a plan. Again her heart pounded—thumping violently against the wall of her chest.

It was light enough to see the path before her when she started out and crossed the clearing with Turbo, heading for the bluff. The grass was wet against her ankles.

When she reached the box elder at the top of the bluff, she commanded Turbo to lie down. Obediently he stretched out on his belly and watched as Ellen hoisted herself up to the dinette chair in the branches above.

She waited there in the box elder until it was light enough down in the ravine below to see the Brody house clearly. It sat as it always had, but listed a little more to the left. Every year it seemed to lean just a bit further, and one end of the porch roof had already caved in.

A white car was parked behind the house, off in the trees. There was no sign of anyone about, and if someone had driven up the Brodys' crooked lane from out on Crow's Point Road, he would have taken one look and called the place deserted.

An hour went by. Then a half-hour longer. Turbo whined once and looked at her; but she spoke to him again, and he hushed.

As the sky brightened, the valley below was clearly focused in the still-subdued light of early morning. The hills were mounds of pure red clay against which evergreens and birches gleamed sharply green and white.

The old house was situated in such a way that Ellen could see it broadside, both front and back porches and the outhouse behind. She waited even longer. She had come prepared to wait. It was Turbo she worried about. She had not dared come without him, but she did not want him barking or wandering off.

And then she saw what she had come for. The back door of the house swung open and a woman stepped cautiously out, looked around, and went back in. A moment later she came out on the porch again, this time holding the hand of a small boy whom she hustled to the outhouse, one hand over his mouth. Jason.

Ellen leaned forward to climb back down again. She would go out to Crow's Point Road and walk the five miles to Dr. George's house. From there they would drive down to Millville and get the sheriff. Phoning the sheriff directly was out of the question. At the first chirp of a call being dialed, Grace Talbot and Mrs. Conklin would listen in. The instant people found out that Jason was being held in the old Brody house, the fields would be swarming with men from around Crow's Point, armed with shotguns. Jason might be killed. Most certainly Gerald would hold him hostage if he were cornered.

Ellen grabbed the rope to swing down when she paused, for Gerald had come out of the house carrying a suitcase and set it down beside the car. The woman appeared again with the child and motioned toward some clothes that were hanging on a makeshift line. She and Gerald seemed to be arguing. Then they both went back inside.

Ellen realized, with a chill that stopped her breath, numbed her brain, that there was no time to go for help. In a few minutes, no more than it took to take clothes off the line, perhaps, Gerald might be gone, and Jason with him.

Fourteen

SHE KNEW what she must do, but the problem was what to do with Turbo. She could not take him with her, yet she wanted him near.

"Turbo," she said to him sternly, pointing: "Stay."

He whined. It was a lot to ask of him, Ellen knew. They had been on the bluff already for two hours. "Stay," she said again, and petted him. He put his head on his paws once more.

The thicket extended just so far, and then there was nothing but tall grass beyond—a long stretch of scrub brush and ribbon grass before Ellen could get to the woods behind the Brody house. When she reached the end of the thicket near the bottom of the ravine, she tied the ends of her old checked shirt tightly around her so they wouldn't drag, got down on her hands and knees, and began to crawl.

On the other side of the woods, beyond the Brody place, was an old field of dead corn, which, since the Brodys left, had become a dumping ground. Boxes and mattresses and newspapers and clothes had piled up, year after year, heap upon heap, until the junction folks found another spot for their trash. Then the old cornfield with its throwaways had been abandoned to the field mice and squirrels once again. This was where

Ellen headed now—first the woods for cover, then the field. She patted her jeans pocket to make sure that the usual matches were there.

It was difficult to judge distance from where she was crawling, low in the grass. Her knees were sore and the palms of her hands burned from the stubble. Every so often she stopped, trying to get her bearings, pushing back the long hair that hung about her face, not daring to raise her head above the top of the ribbon grass.

A door slammed, and Ellen pressed herself to the ground, lying motionless. Dry milkweed filled her nostrils with dust, and she pressed her lips together tightly to keep from sneezing. There were footsteps on the back porch, voices, and then the footsteps went back inside. If only she could reach the field before the car left.

When several minutes had passed and there was no more sound, Ellen continued her slow journey. She felt the earth growing damp beneath her and remembered that she had the creek yet to cross. Inching her way along the bank, she came to a clump of bushes to hide her crossing. She crouched, leaping onto a rock, then a root, but one foot went in with a splash. Ellen waited there on the other side, scarcely breathing. No door opened, however. Nothing. Finally she began the last leg of her journey toward the woods.

It seemed ten minutes before she got there, and her greatest fear was that Turbo would tire of waiting and follow. At last the first tree loomed before her, then another, but it wasn't until she was enveloped in shadow that she allowed herself, aching and sore, to stand up. She wiped one sleeve across her forehead and shoved back her hair once again.

The back door opened and through the trees Ellen

saw Gerald come out. He was examining something in his hands, holding it up to the light, then fidgeting with it some more. A gun. Ellen put one hand hard against her chest to slow her heart. She had come this far; she wouldn't quit.

The woman came to the door.

"What you taking that for?"

"Might need it."

"Girl might see it."

"I'm getting edgy." Gerald rubbed the back of his neck. "I say let's leave."

"'Nother half-hour won't hurt. Time enough to eat. You go get us something. Tell the girl you'll work later."

"Have to wait till she gets up," Gerald said, and went back inside.

Silently Ellen made her way on through the woods, gauging each step, setting her weight down so carefully that she did not snap a twig, rustle a leaf, disturb a branch.

She had no watch, but estimated the time to be about eight-thirty.

Hidden from view of the house, she quickly surveyed the rubbish pile and chose a heap especially full of cardboard boxes. Lifting a dead branch, she quietly placed that on top, then an ancient bundle of magazines and all the dry kindling she could gather in one armload. After each movement she stopped, listening. Then, rearranging the assortment slightly, Ellen set fire to the trash in three places. When she was sure it was blazing well, she rushed into the woods, her heart thumping wildly, lips dry, and made her way back toward the Brody house.

She was afraid for a moment that the fire might have gone out, that things were still wet from the rain earlier that week. But a second later, the smoke reached her nostrils. The back door of the house flew open, and the woman ran out. She was looking toward the field.

"Sam!" she yelled. "A fire!"

Sam?

Hurried footsteps from inside and the door burst open again. Gerald swore, leaped off the porch, grabbing a blanket from off the back railing and started toward the field. Then he ran back suddenly, stuck his head inside, and yelled to someone there, "You *stay* here, you understand? You'll get the beating of your life if you come out this door."

The woman picked up a pail and filled it at the pump, then carried it, water sloshing, behind Gerald.

In an instant Ellen was behind the outhouse and when both Gerald and the woman disappeared around the edge of the woods, she ran up on the porch and opened the back door.

The kitchen was dark and smelled of grease and dirt. A four-year-old boy stood tear-streaked and terrified in one corner.

"Jason," Ellen said. "Come quickly and don't make a sound. I want to help you."

He stared up at her without answering.

She reached out and took his arm, but he edged back against the wall.

"I can't," he whispered, the fear in his voice matching his eyes.

"Please trust me. Your parents want you home."

He started to cry, but she hugged him to her. "Shhhh."

She led him hastily through the dirty rooms to the front door and on out to the tumbledown front porch. She had just started to step off when she saw the woman running across the back yard. This time the woman passed the pump and ran directly to the creek instead, quickly scooping up a bucket of water, then rushing off. She would be back again, Ellen knew. Ellen could not possibly go home the same way she had come.

Holding Jason's hand tightly, she ran down the path leading to the far end of the Stumps's pasture. It was the way Gerald came to work each morning, a longer journey, but level, without the steep bluff to navigate. Soon she and Jason were hidden in trees, the ground beneath them strewn with pine needles. There was a half mile yet to go before they would reach the gate at the back of the pasture. The smoke was still pungent to Ellen's nostrils.

And then she heard what she had feared all along: Turbo's barking. Her heart rose up in her mouth. It was a frenzied bark, and through the trees she could just see him coming down the side of the bluff toward the ravine. He did not come toward her. He rushed instead toward the burning field. The smoke had alarmed him, made him break his watch.

The barking grew more hysterical—then turned to frenzy. A shot rang out, a yelp, and then silence.

"Oh, no!" Ellen cried, her eyes brimming. "Oh, lordy, no!" She stood rooted to the ground, unable to go on, one hand over her mouth.

Jason stared up at her.

"My dog!" Ellen choked, and fear overwhelmed

her. Gerald had shot Turbo and could easily shoot her. She grabbed Jason's hand again and stumbled on, choking and gasping as she ran, letting the tears come.

They neared the property line at last where spindly cedars, their trunks white and knobbed like turkey bones, parted for her at the gate.

Ellen had to go through it to reach the orchard. She could see the horse looking at her from across the pasture, one foot forward, then his body following. Swooping Jason up in her arms, Ellen made a run for the fence that separated pasture from plum and peach trees and dropped him over the rail, then quickly climbed over herself. Sleet followed them along the fence, head tossing.

Ellen realized that this was as far as her plans had taken her. All her energy had gone into figuring out how she would get Jason out of the Brody house, but what now? Should she try to call Dwight Ruggles, and let the neighbors swarm if they wanted? Or should she take Jason out to the road and try to make it to the junction?

When they reached the clearing, however, she heard a new sound, the noise of a car down on Crow's Point Road. And Ellen knew in a way she could not explain that it was Gerald's car, and he was coming for her.

She pushed Jason up on the porch and through the door ahead of her. "He's coming here," she said. "I'm going to hide you until the police come, and you've got to promise you'll be quiet. Not a sound. Not a peep. Can you do it? Can you be that brave?"

He didn't answer. He was shaking.

"*Please* try, Jason," she pleaded. "Please do it for me. I want to help you."

He nodded, his face white.

Frantically she dragged him from room to room looking for a hideout. The noise of the car had stopped, and Ellen knew that Gerald had parked it at the end of the drive. Was he waiting there for her, then?

She thought of the broom closet, the bed, the blanket chest—all places Gerald would look. Desperately she rushed back across the breezeway, and then she thought of the oven. It had been cold for several days.

She opened the door and yanked out the rack, slipping it behind the stove. Gathering up the tablecloth, she stuffed it in as bedding and helped Jason crawl inside. Just as she closed the door, she heard a strange sound, as though someone were climbing up the side of the house. There was a thud on the porch, footsteps. She rushed over and picked up the telephone. The line was dead.

Fifteen

HE STEPPED INSIDE without knocking, her father's hedge clippers in his hand.

"Who you fixing to call?"

Ellen did not see his gun, but she knew he had it on him by the telltale bulge beneath his shirt.

His question gave her the opening that she needed.

"Dr. George," she answered, "but the phone's out. Don't get any ring at all."

"Fancy that," said Gerald. He came a few steps into the room and looked around.

"I can't understand it," Ellen chattered on, struggling to hide her breathlessness. "It was working fine yesterday."

Gerald studied her suspiciously. They were both playing a game, she knew.

"What you want with the doctor? You look like you're better now."

Her mind raced on ahead of her, creating a story. "I am. It's Granny Bo. She's fallen and broken her hip, I think."

Ellen saw the disbelief on his face. Gerald sneered. "Yeah? And how would you know that?"

Ellen was surprised how easily words came to her. "What's wrong with you, Gerald? I swear, everything's at odds this morning. Turbo's wandered off, there's a fire burning somewhere, Granny Bo's broken her hip, and now you're acting like you got up on the wrong side of the bed."

"How do you know she fell?" he insisted.

"Her old mule wandered up here this morning, and I figured something must have happened. I took it back down and sure enough, Granny Bo had fallen off in the yard. I put a pillow under her head and a blanket on top, but I was scared to move her. Somehow Dr. George has got to get an ambulance in there and get her to the hospital."

"Well, she's not likely to die soon, and I got problems, too," Gerald said. "Somebody's got something of mine, and I aim to get it back."

"What is it?"

She tried to move past him, to lure him into the parlor, but he stayed put, and studied her without answering.

"If you'll just *tell* me," Ellen scolded, "without standing there like a deaf man. . . ." She could tell she was playing her part well; Gerald didn't know whether to believe her or not.

"Never you mind," he said. "But I'll have me a look around."

Ellen shrugged. "Go ahead. Can't think of a thing you've got I'd want. Not your disposition, *that's* a fact."

She went to the refrigerator and rummaged about. "Want some breakfast?" she said.

Gerald gave no answer, but began opening the lower cupboards on either side of the sink.

Oh, god, Jason, don't move, she prayed.

Gerald stopped a moment, looking around. His eye fell on the stove and he took a step closer. Then he lifted a few pieces of kindling off the top of the wood box, peered in, and put them back.

"For heaven's sake, Gerald, what on earth do you want?"

He turned and stood with arms folded over his chest. "Can't figure you out," he said. "Don't know if you're lyin' or not."

"About *what*?" Ellen said indignantly.

"Somebody," said Gerald, "set that fire over by the Brody house."

"Is that where it was?" Ellen said. "Then *that's*

where Turbo was off to, barking his head off."

Gerald's eyes never left her face.

***

At that moment, there was the rattle of a bicycle on the lane outside. Gerald whirled around, one hand over the bulge beneath his shirt.

"Who's that?" he said quickly.

"Just a gentle retarded boy who's come to deliver my groceries," said Ellen. "And whatever you're looking for, Gerald, *he* doesn't have it, so don't you give him a hard time."

She flounced past him and went to the door.

"Hi!" Jimmy-Clyde called cheerfully. "Mrs. Gacy said I should come here first thing and bring you the aspirin."

Ellen held the screen open for him, and he stepped inside, then stopped when he saw Gerald.

"Jimmy-Clyde, this is Gerald, who's been helping out around here," Ellen said, taking the sack from him and carrying it out to the kitchen. She eyed the oven door. It was slightly ajar, and then, very slowly, it closed again.

Jimmy-Clyde was still staring at Gerald. "Is that your car out there on the road? You parked right in the middle, and I couldn't hardly get by."

"I'll move it," said Gerald, but made no sign of leaving.

Jimmy-Clyde followed Ellen out to the kitchen and began lifting things from the sack. "Aspirin . . . oranges . . . mayonnaise . . ."

Gerald watched from the doorway. "Okay, okay," he said. "Ellen can do that."

Jimmy-Clyde looked at him, hurt.

"You go on back now," said Gerald.

The boy looked at Ellen imploringly. "I can't see the horse?"

"We pay him to clean out Sleet's stall," Ellen explained to Gerald.

"Well, I'll be doing that today," Gerald said. "We're kind of busy around here, and I'm fixing to shore up a corner of the barn. You go on."

Disappointed, Jimmy-Clyde turned to go, but Ellen stopped him.

"Listen, Jimmy-Clyde." She faced him, her hands on his shoulders, her face as serious as she could make it. "You've got to take a message to Dr. George."

Gerald edged closer, but she paid no attention.

"Granny Bo fell off her mule this morning, and I think she's broken her hip. I want you to go straight back to his office. Okay? And I want you to tell him that Ellen says Granny Bo broke her hip, and he should get an ambulance up from Millville and go get her out. Can you remember all that?"

Jimmy-Clyde's eyes opened wide. "Go back to Gacy's and . . ."

"No. Go straight to Dr. George's, Jimmy-Clyde. And what are you going to tell him?"

"Granny Bo fell off her mule."

"And broke her hip! That's the important part. He's got to get an ambulance in there and take her to the hospital."

"Got to get an ambulance in there and get her out," said Jimmy-Clyde.

"That's right. You won't forget, now?"

"No."

"Promise?"

"I'll go right now. Wow! Big excitement."

Jimmy-Clyde went back out to his bicycle, forgetting Sleet, and pedaled furiously back down the lane.

"He come here often?" Gerald asked.

"Two or three times a week—any time I need something from the store."

"Well, I better go move my car," Gerald said, as Ellen busied herself at the sink. He started to leave, then turned. "I got a feeling that what I'm looking for is right in this house, Ellen. And I aim to sit right here till it shows up, so don't go gettin' any ideas."

"Suit yourself," she said as he left, but as she glanced at herself in the mirror, she saw a sooty smudge on the left side of her face and bits of ash in her hair. Her heart almost stopped. He knew!

She could not keep Jason in the oven any longer. Sooner or later he would move or cry or cough. She could not get out to the road with Gerald coming in, and if she tried to make it down the back path to Granny Bo's, he would catch up with her before she even reached the bluff.

Suddenly Ellen knew where she would hide Jason—the one place Gerald would not look. As soon as she heard his car start at the end of the drive, she opened the oven door.

"Jason," she said to the trembling child who was covered now with soot and grease. "Come with me. Don't make any noise." They ran outside, crossed the clearing and a moment later entered the barn. And

then, with Jason beside her, her terror mounting, Ellen
led him toward Sleet's stall.

❦

It was the most frightening thing Ellen had ever
done in her life. The horse was not there, but every step
she took made her feel as though hooves were poised,
ready to strike her, teeth ready to bite.

Jason began to cry from fatigue.

"It will be better here," Ellen said unconvincingly,
burrowing their way behind the bales of straw that had
been piled in one corner. "Come in here, Jason. This
will be our hideout."

She could hear the sound of Gerald's car heading
back up the lane in first gear, bumping, thumping as
the wheels hit the ruts, springs squeaking. It came to a
stop finally in the clearing, and the door slammed.
Heavy-booted footsteps again, going in the house, and
the sound of a screen door banging.

"I'm afraid," Jason cried, and Ellen hugged him
tightly.

"I won't leave you," she promised. "I'll stay with
you every minute."

"Will Daddy come?"

"Yes. When the police get here."

What Ellen hoped was that when Dr. George and
the rescue squad reached Granny Bo's and found her in
good health, they would know that something was amiss
at Ellen's. If Jimmy-Clyde mentioned the man he saw
standing in Ellen's kitchen, as she hoped he would, that
should bring the police. It was the only thing she could
count on now.

How thin Jason was in her arms, how terribly small and fragile, with the sweaty little-boy smell of a child who hadn't bathed for several days.

He snuggled close against her, and in his blackened clothes looked like a street urchin, a chimney sweep.

"How did you know I was over at their house?" he whispered.

"I heard you cry last night."

"They put their hands over my mouth."

"I heard you anyway."

The screen door slammed, and there were footsteps on the porch once more. "Ellen?"

There was a pause.

Then louder, angrier: "Ellen!" Gerald swore. Jason trembled in Ellen's arms.

A woman's voice came from somewhere out behind the barn in the other direction.

"What's happened?"

"I can't find the girl," Gerald told her.

"Did she make off with him, then?"

"Damned if I know. Thought at first she didn't, but now I'm sure she did. *Blast* it!"

"The fire's out. We'll be lucky if somebody didn't see it and call the trucks."

That was another possibility Ellen hadn't thought of. She began to hope.

"We've got to find Ellen. I know she didn't take the lane out because I was bringing the car in. Go up the back path and see if she's started for the bluff. Won't get very far if she has. Path's steep, and she'll have the kid with her."

The woman's footsteps hurried off again.

A shadow darkened the doorway, but it wasn't Gerald's. Ellen peered timorously out between the bales of straw to see if the woman had by chance come back, and as she did so, the dark horse came inside.

Sixteen

IT SEEMED almost five minutes that the horse stood there, sensing something. Ellen knew that even if Gerald did not see her, all he had to do was take a look at Sleet, at the way he had tensed, and he would guess. She could hear Gerald moving around outside, whacking at bushes with a stick, searching the buckberry thicket. Sleet moved forward at last, slowly, until he could see over the bales of straw, and his huge eye looked down on Ellen, his sleek head seemed to shiver. Ellen shivered, too.

"Is that your horse?" Jason whispered in her ear. She nodded, too terrified to speak.

"We have horses in California," Jason whispered again. "Sometimes they run in races."

Ellen could see Sleet's ears perk up at the whispered sound of Jason's voice.

She hoped that perhaps Jason's scent would mask her own, certain that Sleet could sense her fear. How tall he seemed, looming up over them, the white showing around the dark pupil of his eye. He jerked his head, tossing his mane. Between the orange of his gums, his teeth showed yellow. Ellen could hear the swish of his long tail. The barn seemed filled with demons.

She bent forward, her head on her knees, one hand over the back of her neck as though to protect herself. Fear had caught up with her at last, and the courage she had felt that morning, both at the Brody house and later in her own kitchen, was gone. She was shaking as though it were winter.

Desperately she tried to figure out how much time had passed since Jimmy-Clyde had left. Twenty minutes, perhaps. He would scarcely be back at the junction yet. Then it would take another five minutes to park his bike and go across the street to see Dr. George. She wondered if Jimmy-Clyde would sit patiently in Dr. George's waiting room. She had forgotten to tell him to go up to the examining room door and knock— to tell the doctor it was an emergency. *Oh, god. . . .*

There were voices outside again.

"Did you find her?"

A curse from Gerald. "No."

"Well, she isn't on the back path. I followed it down to where I could see a good long stretch, and she wasn't anywhere about. Searched the rocks around. I think she's sneaked past you and gone out to the road, through the garden or someplace."

"Don't see how she could. Vines so heavy it's like a wall all about the place. She'd have to have a macheté to get through, and I'd have heard her tramping around. She's here some place, and I aim to find her. Dottie, you stand in the yard so she can't make a run for it either way."

The heavy boots were coming toward the barn. Ellen crouched down even further, pulling Jason with her.

"Shhhh," she said, as she felt his small body shake.

The footsteps were in the barn, coming closer to the stall. Sleet moved away toward the railing as Gerald appeared. There was a pause again, a longer one. The thumping in Ellen's chest grew so loud she was sure Gerald could hear it. Finally, however, the footsteps went back out.

"You look around in there real good?" the woman asked.

"Horse is in there. She won't go near it. Got the crazies about that animal bein' some kind of devil." And then he yelled: "Ellen? I know you're here someplace, and I aim to find you. You come out, I'll go easy on you. You cost me any more time lookin', you'll be sorry you ever did. You hear me?"

Ellen closed her eyes.

"All I want is the boy," he yelled again. "Bring him to me, and I'll let you go."

I'll just bet you would, Ellen thought. He sure must think she was some kind of dumb. But the one-way conversation chilled her, and the fear welled up higher, tickling the back of her throat. Gerald went on:

"Your father's not coming back till Sunday, and you know it, Ellen. You lied to me! You've done a lot of lyin', and I don't take to that, you hear? Bring me the boy, and I'll forget the lyin'. I'm not going to hurt him. You, neither."

Ellen pressed her cheek against Jason's, one finger to her lips.

She lost all track of time. She did not know if ten

more minutes had passed or thirty. If Dr. George and the ambulance had reached Granny Bo's, would the sheriff be here by now? If anyone had seen the smoke, would the fire truck have come? And then Ellen felt her strength give way. It was Thursday, Dr. George's day off. The office would be closed.

Ellen glanced around in despair, too exhausted to think, and found herself looking once more into the eyes of the horse. Sleet had not, after all, given them away.

Leaning against the side of the stall, she let her arms go limp, immobilized now by the fear of Gerald and his gun. No one would know. No one would come. It was all up to her. The horse peered down, shifted, then stood sideways, his eye on Ellen and Jason.

She studied him with a feeling of surrender. One fear had numbed the other. She was afraid of everything, and she was afraid of nothing.

There was something about the droop of his head, the slant of his neck, that made her sense in him her own isolation. When had she ridden Sleet last? She could not remember—could not recall when she had even touched the mane of this devil horse, stroked his flank.

For just one moment, the smell of his warm breath, his body, reminded her of the evening rides she used to enjoy through wet clover out in the meadow—the clop of his hooves, the rhythm of his strong body, his curious wheezy snort of pleasure. But then she thought of Billy and turned her face away.

Still . . .

She could hear the house doors slamming as Gerald paced up and down the breezeway, hear him call her name, swear, and call again.

Slowly, so slowly that her arm ached, Ellen reached up one hand, inch by inch, until it was within a few inches of the horse's nose. She held it there, waiting. Sleet stood very still, his neck muscles tense. He snorted and tossed his head to one side, and his mouth grazed her fingers.

Ellen withdrew her hand. Then timidly, she reached up again. Once more he tossed his head, but this time sniffed her fingers.

On the third try, he held his head still. He sniffed, then sniffed again.

And in her mind's eye Ellen saw her father's face as distinctly as she had seen it after the night cry, as clearly as though he were standing there beside her, and she remembered his words: *What you got to learn is when to doubt and when to trust. . . .*

"Dorothy," she heard Gerald say to the woman. "I think I'll drive out to the road and take a look just in case she *did* slip by me somehow. If she did, she won't be more'n a mile or so either direction, and there ain't a house within five she could go to."

Ellen sat up, listening. Her heart began to pound. Her mind raced.

"I don't much like stayin' here by myself," the woman told him.

"Won't take me more'n ten minutes to run both ways. You see that girl, you hold her down till I come. She's got the boy with her, you just hold onto him. If she *is* here, though, she won't come out, you can bet. When I get back, I'm going over every inch of the place, see where she's hiding."

Ellen listened to the sound of the engine starting, then the slow grinding noise as the car moved back down the lane in low gear, the thud of the wheels as they slipped into the ruts, the clank of the undercarriage.

Now. With shaking legs, Ellen stood up and slowly, slowly, held out both hands. Sleet sniffed them again. She spoke to him softly in a sort of croon, repeating his name over and over. He stood very still, listening. Then, as her father had once taught her to do when a horse was shy, she bent toward him and blew gently on his nostrils.

Could he sense her own loneliness and regret, she wondered? Along with her fear, could he detect her need for him, her dependence? Still crooning softly, too softly for the woman outside to hear, Ellen leaned forward and blew again. The short, deeply arched ears that had been bent back before moved forward as he felt her breath on his face.

"Sleet," she whispered. "Please help me."

She could tell the way his body quivered that he relished her touch, welcomed her breath once more. But there was no time to test him further. Holding onto his mane with one hand, she reached up and lifted the dusty bridle off the wall and slipped it over his head. Gently, gently, she eased the bit into his mouth, then buckled the straps. There was no time for the saddle. Any moment the car could return, and it was Gerald who had the gun.

"We're leaving," she said to Jason, and hoisted him up. "Hang onto his mane."

Sleet stood quietly, willingly receiving his passenger. Ellen softly opened the gate to the stall, then climbed up on the railing and slid on in back of the child.

"Sleet," Ellen whispered, "please do this for me."

She jiggled the reins, and the horse began moving out the opening. He started to turn left toward the pasture, but Ellen guided him to the front door of the barn, which Gerald had left ajar.

◆§§◆

"Hold on tightly, Jason," she whispered, her arms on either side of the boy, reins in hand. Then, gently squeezing her legs against Sleet's ribs, she said, "Go, boy."

The horse trotted out of the barn, and immediately, at Ellen's urging, broke into a gallop.

The woman was standing by the rock garden, her back to the barn, watching the house. Hearing the hoofbeats, she whirled about, gasped, and reached out one arm as though to stop them.

"You, there!" she shouted. "Come on back here! Sam! Sam!"

"Go, boy," Ellen said again, and the horse galloped even faster, across the clearing and on up the path toward the bluff.

There was yelling back in the clearing, the shouts of the woman, the sound of Gerald's car returning, the screech of brakes, and the slam of a door, but Ellen didn't look back. On Sleet went, past the sweet olive tree, on past the bamboo, until at last he had reached the top of the bluff and started down the other side.

A shot rang out and then another. Sleet startled, but did not bolt. The dark coat glistened as he clambered over the rocks, making his way down the steep incline.

"Good boy, good boy," Ellen murmured, patting his neck reassuringly, and guided him between the boulders toward the gentler slope below.

Jason did not speak at all. His hands were white where he gripped Sleet's mane, body rigid with terror.

"You're doing fine, Jason," she told him. "Just hang on."

Her own fears rose again when they reached the place where the ginseng grew. No one had ridden Sleet since that day, least of all here. A horse, it was said, never forgot. What an irony it would be if, after all of this, Sleet should bolt again.

Whether the horse sensed it or Ellen only imagined it, she could feel his body move more jerkily beneath her weight, feel him shy off to one side. He whinnied. The phrase "old man Keat" came to mind, but Ellen allowed it no room. She would give that story back to Granny Bo and let it die out with her. What Sleet did now was up to him, not a devil.

"Good boy," she said again, to show her faith. And a minute later they had passed the ginseng and the fateful rock, and the rolling hills stretched out before them.

Sleet broke into a gallop again, mane flying, sides heaving with the unaccustomed weight. On past grapevine thick as an arm, through briars and fern and thistle, until Granny Bo's cabin came into view, and there was Dr. George's car beside the ambulance and sheriff's cruiser.

Bodies turned, faces stared aghast, hands reached up to stop the horse and help Jason off, then Ellen.

"Lord a mercy, it's the Cory kid!" Dwight Ruggles said.

And finally Ellen stood with trembling legs there on the ground, her arms around Sleet's neck, weeping with relief and joy.

Seventeen

"I JUST RADIOED a car up to your place, Ellen April," Dwight Ruggles told her. "Should be there about now. Who's up there? Who's that man Jimmy-Clyde was tellin' us about?"

Ellen sat down weakly on Granny Bo's steps, glad for Dr. George's strong arm around her shoulder. Alma Goff sat quiet and pale on the step above her.

"He calls himself Gerald Hawkes—says he's one of Ison Hawkes's sons—but a woman with him calls him Sam."

Granny Bo sucked in her breath.

"Can't be one of Ison Hawkes's boys," the ambulance driver said. "We pulled those boys from the river three years back. Both of 'em drowned."

Ellen looked at Granny Bo. The old woman sat with head down, shoulders bent, hands hanging loosely between her knobby knees.

"Just a man and woman up there? Anyone else?" Dwight Ruggles questioned.

"No, but Gerald's got a gun."

The radio inside the sheriff's car began to squawk, and Dwight Ruggles slid back in the front seat and pressed a button.

"What you got, Don?"

"There's a white Ford parked up here at the Stumps', Tennessee license plates."

"That his car, Ellen?" Dwight Ruggles asked.

She nodded.

"Listen," Dwight said into his radio. "That man's armed, and there's a woman with him. I'm sending another car right up. Man's wanted for kidnapping, but the boy's safe."

"The Cory kid?" the voice asked.

"That's right. Don't you let them slip by now, or I'll never hear the end of it."

The radio went off, then came on again as Dwight Ruggles called the county police for another car. "And tell Robert Cory his son is safe, we're bringing him down," he added.

"What happened now, Ellen?" the doctor encouraged.

"I heard a cry . . . a night . . . a cry in the night, and it sounded like a little child." Ellen looked over to where the ambulance driver was opening a can of 7-Up for Jason.

"It was me," said Jason. "They covered up my mouth."

"It sounded as though it was coming from the old Brody place, so I . . ."

"The Brody place!" said Dwight Ruggles, slapping his knee. "Why didn't *I* think of that?"

Ellen went on. As they waited for news on the sheriff's radio, she told them how she had seen the woman come out of the house with Jason, how she had set the fire, but when she came to the part about Turbo being shot, she choked up and covered her face with her hands, crying silently, the tears seeping through the cracks between her fingers. Jason came over and leaned against her as she finished her tale.

"Sam . . ." said Granny Bo, as if to herself.

"When can I see my daddy?" Jason asked.

"Soon, honey," Ellen told him, drying her eyes on her shirt. "Why don't you help me fill a bucket of water for my horse?"

She got the mule's bucket and filled it from Granny Bo's rain barrel. Together, she and Jason carried it over and set it on the ground. The horse slurped lustily, and when he was through, held his tongue lightly between his teeth as droplets of water pattered down on the grass below, a funny little habit Ellen had long forgotten.

"Sleet," she said, and pressed her cheek against him.

The radio came on again.

"It's over," the voice said. "Sam Goff surrendered—him and a woman named Dorothy Cray."

Sam Goff? Alma's son? Ellen turned around. Dr. George was patting Granny Bo on the shoulder.

"It wasn't your fault, Alma. You did the best you could. Sam's a grown man."

"Sam's dead," the old woman said.

Dwight Ruggles and the ambulance driver exchanged glances.

"We've got to take Ellen to town with us to make a statement," Dr. George said to Granny Bo. "Can she leave her horse here until we bring her back?"

The old woman nodded.

"Will you be all right, Alma?"

Granny Bo nodded again.

"Listen," Ellen said to Dwight Ruggles. "Tell the police to go in my house and bring out the tablet of paper on my Dad's desk. The pen, too. It will have fingerprints on it, I'm sure."

Dwight Ruggles relayed the message on the radio.

"Anything else you want brought down?" the radio squawked back.

"What else you got?"

"Nothing much, 'cept a half-dead dog with a wound in his leg."

"Turbo!" cried Ellen, jumping to her feet. "That's my dog! He's alive!"

"Tell them to bring that dog down to my office," said Dr. George. "And handle him gently."

It was a strange procession that made its way through the long tangle of weeds and ribbon grass out to the dead-end road, then on to Crow's Point Road, and down to Millville. First Dwight Ruggles in the sheriff's car, then the ambulance, and finally Dr. George and Ellen with Jason between them, his head on Ellen's lap.

"Why does Granny Bo say her son is dead when he's not?" Ellen asked.

Dr. George sighed. "Sam was her youngest and a real trial to her. She reached a point, I guess, where it was easier to believe him dead than getting in all the trouble he did, so the last time he went off, she told herself that he died. And finally, she almost came to believe it."

"But what did he have against Robert Cory?"

"Well, it's speculation on my part, but thirteen years ago, before Cory left for California, he hired Sam Goff as horse trainer and handyman, and I think the understanding was that when he moved west, he'd take Sam with him. Well, Sam's troubles caught up with him—his bad checks and all the rest—and instead of taking Sam along, Cory fired him. Guess Sam never forgave him for that."

Jason moved a little on Ellen's lap, but when she looked down, she saw that his eyes were closed. His lips spluttered as he slept. She stroked his cheek, still sooty from her oven.

"Gerald—I mean, Sam—was a hard worker, Dr. George, did lots of things about our place. It's hard to believe he was born bad."

"He wasn't," said the doctor. "No more than your horse was born spooked. There's a whole list of charges against Sam Goff, and he's probably guilty of every one of them, but I can't forget that years ago, when he was about sixteen, he walked all the way up to my place carrying a friend on his back who had hurt himself bad. Maybe we'll never know what it was started him off wrong."

Ellen leaned against the car window, drinking in

the scent of lilies, the sight of willows heavy with clumps of muscadine vine, the mimosa. She had made her peace at last with Sleet, and Turbo was alive. In her joy, she almost overlooked something else—something unseen and unspoken but so heavy she could almost hold it in her hand.

Coincidence of place and time and weather on the day Billy died had caused her to change a horse once loved into a demon undeserving of charity or forgiveness. Gossip about a lonely old woman had made her afraid of Granny Bo and her stories. And finally, resentment at her father's leaving had allowed Ellen to suspect the man she cared about more than anyone else in the world.

The procession entered Millville, and there were already people standing out on the sidewalk, staring. A man with a camera came running.

Dr. George parked behind Dwight Ruggles's car in front of the sheriff's office, where Mr. and Mrs. Cory waited anxiously on the sidewalk.

"You're back, Jason," Ellen said, as he sat up, groggy from his nap.

The Corys flung themselves toward the car. In a blur of beige suit and green dress, they pulled Jason out across Ellen's lap. Tears. Hugs. And then they were hugging Jason and Ellen together.

Spectators pressed forward, a group of cameramen intervened. Microphones were thrust toward Robert Cory and his wife. Soon they were separated from Ellen by a hedge of cameras and cables.

"You'll have to come inside and make a statement,

Ellen, and then I'll drive you back to Granny Bo's," the doctor said, taking her arm.

Ellen started toward the door of the station when someone put a hand on her shoulder and gently turned her around. It was Maureen Sinclair. Ellen drew back startled.

"You're Ellen Stump, aren't you?" the woman was saying, her beautiful eyes smiling. She was talking to Ellen but speaking into a small microphone she held in one hand. "Ellen, I know you're anxious to go inside and get this over with, but would you have just a moment to tell our viewers about that fantastic rescue of Jason Cory?"

A WMER camera moved in for a closer view, and Ellen was struck dumb. Microphones were extended toward her face. She shook her head, embarrassed. She could not take her eyes off Maureen Sinclair. Maureen Sinclair in person, so polished and poised and perfectly groomed. Then she glanced down and focussed on her own sooty arms, her smudged shirt, her faded jeans. . . . Oh, lordy, she must look a mess.

But Maureen Sinclair was speaking into the microphone again: "For the past thirty minutes, about as long as it took you to get down here, Ellen, we've been listening to an account of the rescue as it was coming in over the sheriff's radio. I've never met you before, but if someone had told me to paint a picture of the heroine of this story, I would have drawn her exactly like you. You look just the way I hoped you would—every bit the heroine. What was going through your mind when you set out this morning to find Jason?"

Ellen, her face burning, stood with head down, tongue-tied.

"To have carried this out all by yourself, with no help from anyone else . . ." Maureen went on encouragingly.

"It wasn't like that," Ellen mumbled.

"Excuse me?" Maureen Sinclair stepped closer and moved the microphone within inches of Ellen's lips.

Ellen looked around desperately, praying for the woman with the beautiful eyes to go away, for the cameras to focus on Robert Cory again. And then she caught sight of Jimmy-Clyde standing off in the crowd, beaming at her, his pink tongue flicking in and out between his teeth. How proud he was of her. What a big moment this was for him.

"There's . . . there's somebody ought to be standing here with me," Ellen said softly. "I see him right over there."

Maureen Sinclair turned, and the cameras whirred away, scanning the crowd.

"Jimmy-Clyde," Ellen motioned. "Come over here and get yourself on television."

In delighted bewilderment, Jimmy-Clyde came forward and stood beside Ellen, grinning at her.

And then, not looking at the cameras but at Jimmy-Clyde, as though she were talking only to him, Ellen related the story, of how she had hidden Jason and sent Jimmy-Clyde to the junction for help. Jimmy-Clyde's eyes opened wide at the thought of Jason in the oven, but he listened quietly, interlocking his pudgy fingers in front of him, then putting his hands in his pockets and flicking his tongue once more.

Ellen paused suddenly. "Jimmy-Clyde, Dr. George wasn't even supposed to be in his office today. How on earth did you find him?"

Jimmy-Clyde smiled broadly. "I went around to the house and knocked," he said. "I banged the door." Ellen threw her arms around him and hugged him hard, oblivious of the cameras that were humming away.

Bit by bit, with Maureen Sinclair's gentle prodding, the events came out and, at the end, Ellen was able to face the camera herself and finish the story.

When the interview was over, Maureen Sinclair squeezed Ellen's arm. "I hope, if I'm ever called on to be courageous, that I will carry it off as well as you did, Ellen. It was a real pleasure to meet you."

"Well, I can hardly believe I'm meeting *you*," Ellen told her. "I watch *News at Noon* every day—I did until the TV went out, I mean. I still watch it, without the sound. When you tell about something happening, over in Europe and everything, it's just like I was there."

The reporter looked at her intently. "Listen, Ellen, I would be so pleased if you would come down to the studio and have lunch with me next week. It would be a real privilege to introduce you to the others."

Ellen grinned. She couldn't help herself. "I can't believe this is happening," she said.

"Well, none of us can quite believe how brave you were this morning. I'll call you next Monday, and we'll set up a date."

The woman went back to the WMER van, and Ellen turned to Jimmy-Clyde.

"You know who else is a real hero?" she said. "Sleet. And he's going to be so happy to see you again." Jimmy-Clyde seemed drunk with smiling.

"Phone call for Ellen Stump," someone shouted from the door of the sheriff's office.

Ellen made her way over to the door and went inside.

"Ellen!" It was her father's voice. "Honey, I been callin' all over creation for you. The phone didn't ring at home—the line's down, they tell me. I been hearin' all kinds of things on the car radio and drivin' like crazy, stopping ever' chance I got to call. Are you all right, honey? Are you really all right?"

"I'm fine, Dad," Ellen said, choking up. And then, "Please come home."

"I'm on my way. Won't take my foot off the gas till I'm up on Crow's Point Road."

A mockingbird sang in the darkness from somewhere on top of the house. He went through his repertoire of catbird calls and whippoorwills and sparrows, and then started all over again.

Ellen carried the plates to the sink while her father sat cutting a big yellow apple in pieces, his broad thumb over the stem.

"When did Mr. Cory say he was coming, Dad?" Ellen asked.

"Just Saturday . . . didn't say exactly what time."

"Think I'll be gone when he gets here," Ellen mused.

"You're goin' to be waitin' right here, little gal. Wouldn't be polite not to."

Ellen came back to the table and rested one knee on her chair. "What we going to do with that reward money, Dad? Everybody keeps asking. I tell them we don't go around thinking what to do with something we never expected to get."

"I figure we won't have to sit up nights worryin' how to put it to use," her father said. "Isn't one square inch on this property don't need fixing up somehow, and you got to decide if you want to go to the junior college. That'll do for a start, I reckon."

Ellen went back to the sink again and began scrubbing at the plates. "It's embarrassing is what it is. Wasn't one ounce of courage in me, Dad. I was scared as a polecat up a tree over a river."

"That's what I mean," said her father. "You were scared half out of your mind, but you went and did it anyways."

Turbo came limping into the kitchen with a bandaged leg, and Ellen fed him scraps from supper. "What do you suppose will happen to Gerald, Dad?" she asked, as she scratched Turbo's ears. "To Sam, I mean?"

"Dwight Ruggles says that after he goes on trial here, he'll have to face charges for armed robbery in Tennessee. Don't know he'll ever be out of jail after serving all the time he's got coming. Him and that woman, too."

"Did Granny Bo know he was around, do you suppose?"

"Might have suspected it, with feelin's like there was between him and Cory; but she probably kept the worries even from herself."

"Dad . . ." Ellen had to tell him; she couldn't go on keeping it in. She straightened up slowly and turned toward her father, facing the back of his head: "For a while, before I knew it was Gerald did it, I thought maybe, somehow, you were mixed up in the kidnapping." Her face burned.

Joe turned slowly and studied her. "Me, Ellen April?"

"Everything just got all messed up in my head," Ellen said, tears springing to her eyes. "People started asking me questions—where you had gone, how come you took off. . . . Then I saw that writing tablet and pen. . . . Maybe I was angry that you left me alone, and I just took coincidence and turned it into something awful."

He smiled at her then. "Seems like there's a lot of that goin' around lately. Don't think no more about it, honey. Just something catching is all." He leaned his long arms on the table and rubbed the back of his neck, head bent. "I'm home now, and I'm going to think twice about ever leaving you here alone. Not right sure I was meant to sell calendars anyways. All those fancy ideas—none of 'em worked out. But somethin' else'll come along. Always has."

She hugged him. Hard.

Had she lived here so long, so closed off from others, that she had started to shut out those she loved best? No, she decided, it wasn't a question of where she lived but of what she allowed her mind to be: hemmed in by superstition or open to the world around her.

⁂

Ellen went out just before dusk to take Sleet for a ride in the meadow. Gently she lifted the bolt on the barn door, saying his name aloud. Then she made her way toward the stall near the back.

The dark horse stood in shadow, watching her

come. He lifted one hoof in anticipation and bobbed his head.

"Hello, boy," she said, and held out a slice of her father's apple. Sleet gingerly accepted it from her fingers and juggled it about on his tongue, mashing it against the roof of his mouth. He wheezed with pleasure.

Ellen took the bridle from the wall and slipped it over his head, careful not to make any sudden movements, talking to him all the while. Things weren't quite the way they used to be. Sleet was still shy, but she could wait. It had taken her a year after Billy's death to trust him again, and now it was her turn to be patient.

Climbing up on the rail, Ellen lowered herself down on the horse's back, and they went out into the pasture. The landscape had a fresh, new look, as though Ellen were seeing her life from a different perspective. Sitting high on Sleet's back, she even spied a thrush's nest she hadn't known was there.

She thought about the date she would make with Maureen Sinclair the following week and felt a small sweep of excitement. She wasn't at all sure she ever wanted to leave Crow's Point—for good, that is. But the important thing was, if she stayed—like Dr. George had stayed all these years—it would be because she really wanted to, and if she left, there was someone to show her how.

She let the reins hang loosely, allowing Sleet to choose his own path. There would be no wild gallop tonight, just a quiet reunion of old friends. The wind blew softly, carrying with it the fragrance of ripe plums there on the ground, the hint of a new September.

Just as they turned around in the far corner of the field, Ellen heard a night cry. She listened as it came again. It might be a young raccoon, she thought, with its cry like a human baby. But she was content, for now, not to know what it was without trying to make up an answer.

The dark horse tossed his head eagerly as the breeze fanned his nostrils, and Ellen patted his neck. She would ride him again tomorrow. Tomorrow she would pick the last of the buckberries and take them to Granny Bo.